EXPERIMENTAL LECTURE

BY

COLONEL SPANKER

ON

The exciting and voluptuous pleasures to be derived
from crushing and humiliating the spirit of a beautiful and modest young lady; as delivered by him
in the assembly-room of the Society of
Aristocratic Flagellants, Mayfair.

———

BIRCHGROVE PRESS

http://www.birchgrovepress.com

ISBN:
978-0-9870956-1-9

Experimental Lecture by Colonel Spanker was first published in London in 1878-79 with the false imprint date 1836. Only 75 copies of the first edition were issued. It was probably written and published by William Lazenby. This edition is based on an 1894 reprint that was printed privately, ostensibly in London: a larger duodecimo bound in black buckram with plain endpapers. Edited by Mark McDougal for Birchgrove Press.

A French translation of *Experimental Lecture, Conférence Expérimentale par le Colonel Cinglant*, was published in Amsterdam in 1886 by Augustin Brancart with a false place of publication, LONDRES, and date, MDCCCLXXX, printed on the title page. It is also available from Birchgrove Press.

CONTENTS

EXPERIMENTAL LECTURE

BY

COLONEL SPANKER

INTRODUCTION

Those of my readers who have perused the revelations of Birchington House, will recognise in our lecturer an enthusiastic apostle of the rod, who, after his voluptuous amusements at the house of Mrs. Smart, returned to London when her establishment was broken up in consequence of the unpleasant enquiries that were beginning to be made after the Misses Bellasis and Sutton, who had been their victims.

Colonel Spanker soon associated himself with two or three gentlemen who had the same penchant for the exercise of the birch, and, by their united efforts, succeeded in forming the Society of Aristocratic Flagellants, which included at least half a dozen of the most beautiful and fashionable ladies of the day.

Their first care was to rent a house in Mayfair just out of Park Lane. Their housekeeper was an old bawd who was well paid to take care of the place, and after letting in the company she always took care to keep out of the way, hearing and seeing nothing.

The gallant Colonel worked upon a well considered system at first, so as gradually to educate the lady members till they were all as ready as himself to go to any extremes in order to develop the highest pitch of voluptuous excitement: he began by securing hired victims, young girls out of the streets, such as match-and-flower-sellers, who for a few guineas were very glad to submit their vulgar buttocks to such whippings as the Colonel at first treated the members to.

The want of modesty and sensibility in such roughly brought up girls was a sad drawback, as the master of the ceremonies had continually explained to his company that only real young ladies thoroughly understood the degradation of being exposed and humiliated before members of their own sex, and what must they feel when they find themselves degraded and punished before a gentleman?

They got into their power a milliner's apprentice who was a great improvement on the vulgar East End girls they had previously experimented upon, but even her blushes and screams did not come up to the Colonel's ideal of a modest sensitive victim, who would afford them an exquisite treat, by her exhibition of blushing sensitiveness at every little exposure, and her final horror and disgust as she thoroughly realises all the shameful indignities to which she is compelled to submit.

These frequent allusions to the insipidity of the pleasures they derived from practising on paid and consenting victims, at length so worked upon the imaginations of his hearers, that they all became quite anxious to secure a fitting sacrifice, and deputed their president to try and secure a pretty young lady with real blue blood in her veins, who had been brought up with every care and tenderness, and thoroughly imbued with every modest sensibility, which a careful and religious training would have made part of her nature.

He explained to them that for some time past he had been using all his energies and persuasion to bring about this unanimous desire for a more heightened and exquisite kind of flagellation, also that already he has had his eye on a young lady well known to most of them, Miss Julia Ponsonby, a lovely young blonde of seventeen, whose widowed mother being compelled to go abroad for a time, is seeking for a suitable lady to whose charge she can entrust her daughter during her absence, adding that he has instructed an instrument of his, in fact a swell gay lady who being rather sly is willing to undertake the business of procuress to the society; this person is to represent herself to Lady Ponsonby as a Miss Carr Burton and furnished with first-rate testimonials (of course forged) he hopes she will be able to secure Julia for them.

A general clapping of hands greets this information whilst the ladies seem to evince even greater anxiety than the gentlemen for accomplishment of their wishes, such exclamations as: "How nice! What a delicious idea! Only to think of having the pretty Julia's bottom, why it will blush like her face! Oh! Colonel dear, we hope, we shan't be disappointed of such a little delicate duck for a victim!" assuring him that all were now as thoroughly interested as he could wish them to be. Thus encouraged he fixed upon an evening in the next week when he felt almost certain to have Miss Julia in his power, and promised to give them a lecture upon the sublime Theory of Flagellation in all its various and delicious aspects, and to illustrate it upon the beautiful victim before him.

THE LECTURE HALL

The Lodge of the Society was a spacious mansion, with an enclosed court before the entrance, so that carriages setting down visitors were not subject to the observation of persons in the street, and victims, who were always brought in closed conveyances, would find it quite impossible to recognise the place again. It is not necessary to describe all the luxurious arrangements of this mansion, but the lecture-hall or place of punishment was a large conservatory, which the Colonel had constructed on to the back of the mansion and covered in with a double glass roof, in order to prevent the escape of sounds and cries; entering this place by marble steps from the back drawing room the visitor would find himself in a kind of crystal palace the roof of which was as high as the house, the two ends and outer side being fitted with palm trees and other luxuriant exotics, enclosing the centre space in a perfect grove of dense foliage and delicious flowering plants and shrubs, all the back windows of the house looked into this kind of eastern paradise, which was alive with parrots, peacocks, and a variety of birds either remarkable for their voice or plumage.

The centre space before mentioned was large as a commodious drawing room, being surrounded on every side by a trellis-work to which was trained quite a hedge of beautiful prickly cactus in full blossom. At one end a powerful fountain threw up its refreshing sprays, whilst the gold fish sported in a capacious basin at its foot, the other end was arranged with about a dozen luxurious chairs and a table for refreshments, whilst in the centre stood an old-fashioned Berkeley horse, a thing to secure the victims to, so that they could be arranged at any desired angle, or even suspended so as not to touch the floor with their toes, it was something like a large pair of steps, only made of mahogany, the foot board and edges being padded and covered with red baize.

The last thing to mention is the floor which was a most tasteful display of coloured tiles, the mosaic of which made it look as if strewed with gathered flowers.

The assumed Miss Carr Burton is quite successful in her scheme for getting Miss Julia Ponsonby into her power, having represented herself to Lady Ponsonby as living in apartments at Hampton Court Palace; but that she will take a house for the season in Mayfair and act as guardian and chaperone to the dear Miss Julia.

Lady Ponsonby is delighted with the arrangement so much to her daughter's advantage, and on the day she is leaving for the continent, she entrust her beautiful Julia to Miss Carr Burton, who says they will first go over the house in Mayfair which is being prepared for them, and then go down to her apartments for a few days. The mamma departs in blissful happiness at having everything so comfortably settled, and then the brougham (hired of course) of Miss Carr Burton took that Lady and her cortege to the house near Park Lane.

They find an elegant dinner set out in the dining room, to which the two ladies do ample justice, waited on by a demure looking femme de chamber, whom the old housekeeper has got to assist her. After a while Miss Carr Burton gives orders for the brougham to be prepared to take them to Hampton Court, and say she must write a note, and perhaps her dear Julia would like to look over the bedroom and boudoir being specially prepared for her, asking Mary to show Miss Ponsonby the way. Julia is delighted with the rooms, but is suddenly alarmed to find herself alone, and the door locked, the French woman has locked her in, it is beginning to get dusk, presently a note is slipped under the door. Julia snatches it up and hastens to light the candle on her dressing table, the note runs as follows:—

"My dear Miss Ponsonby,

Excuse any seeming treachery, but I am not what you suppose, Carr Burton is an assumed name supported by false representations. I am compelled to go home, but it is not Hampton Court. You will find yourself under the guardianship of a nice gentleman, who has employed me to get you into his power, he will be a real parent to you and make you acquainted with wholesome fatherly discipline. You are wanted as a subject to lecture upon before a society of ladies and gentlemen, who meet in this house for the practice of flagellation; they are members of the same aristocratic society in which you have been accustomed to move. They know you quite well, but will be so disguised as to be unrecognizable to you. Prepare yourself, poor dear Julia, for all sorts of exposures, whippings, and humiliations. Their pleasure in watching your exquisite sufferings, will prevent the least sympathy for their beautiful tender victim. My part of the plot is accomplished, and in bidding you adieu, I hasten to leave a house where lady visitors stand too much upon their dignity to tolerate the presence of their procuress."

A deadly pallor came over the face of the frightened girl as the note dropped from her fingers. She threw herself upon her knees by the side of the bed, her hands clasped in agony, as she exclaimed: "Oh! Oh! Oh, God! Have mercy upon me, and deliver me from this awful peril;" but their was no comfort for the poor girl, as the reality of her imprisonment seemed more apparent every moment, the room was seemingly filled with her sobs, sighs and moans, as she buried her face in the feather bed.

She did not hear the stealthy step of a military looking gentleman, who silently emerged from a closet in one corner of the room, he was a fine looking man about fifty five, with a greyish moustache, bald head, and thick bushy eyebrows, which gave his ruddy cheeks a very severe expression when he was at all angry. For a few minutes he stood behind the poor miserable young Lady, rubbing his hands, and gloating over her with a most pleased expression, reminding one of a satyr who has surprised a sleeping nymph.

It was the Colonel, at length he exclaimed in a rather rough tone: "Miss Ponsonby, will you do me the honour of rising, and allow your new guardian to introduce himself."

Julia. — "Oh! It is true? I dare not look up."

Colonel. — "Stand up this instant, young lady; look me in the face, and see if I am not a man to be obeyed."

Julia. — "Mercy! Mercy! Let me go home; how cruel to be thus entrapped!"

A sudden courage seems to come to her assistance, and she springs to her feet, stamping her pretty boots on the floor in impotent rage, as she brushes back her golden locks, and displays to the Colonel's delighted gaze, her crimson face and red streaming eyes, as she says with an agonized and impassioned tone: "Is it true, sir, that you have got me in your power, that my miserable sufferings may amuse yourself and friends?..."

She had evidently intended to say much more, but her first look in the Colonel's face seemed too freeze the blood in her veins, which had the moment before been boiling with indignation.

"Ha! ha! ha!" said the Colonel, with a brutal laugh. "How do you like the look of me for a guardian? Mark my words, Miss Julia Ponsonby, I am a man to be obeyed, if I only lift up my little finger. Are you prepared to promise the most implicit obedience in every thing I order, even if it is to strip yourself naked."

Julia, blushing up to the roots of her hair, seems dazed and bewildered, but after a slight hesitation, her tongue gives vent to her indignation. "No! no! no! sir, I would die first, you can never compel me to do that."

Colonel fiercely seizes the young lady by her wrist and drags her a few steps, till he sinks into an armchair. "Now, girl," he hisses in her ear, "you are in my power, will you kiss me, and promise obedience?"

Shriek after shriek escapes the poor agonized girl as she wrestles and struggles to get away from his iron grasp.

Colonel, angrily, with knitted brows: "Ah! I see what sort of a girl I have to deal with, you must have a lesson at once;" throwing her body across her knees.

"Oh! Oh! My God! For heaven's sake, sir, what are you about?" shrieks out Julia, ready to die with shame and indignation, as she feels her petticoats thrown over her head, and knows there is nothing but her drawers to prevent him from seeing her naked bottom. His hands fall in with four tremendous smacks, each one quite suspending the breath of the struggling girl.

"Ah! We can feel a little, can we, Miss Julia, lucky for you that I have no rod handy, or your delicate skin might get cut up the first night you are under my roof, but my hand can do no harm. I'll just open your drawers a little behind, and see if a few slaps on your naked flesh will make you more obedient."

Julia is horrified, disgusted, and ready to die with shame.

The Colonel uncovers her head a little to enjoy the sight of her blushing face, and starting terrified eyes: "Ha! Ha! Miss Ponsonby, yours is a pretty bottom, not too fat, quite a refined exhibition for a modest young lady," says he. "How do you like that! And that!! And that!!! How deliciously your white skin flushes under my smashes, we shall have a most exquisite lecture to-morrow; you are just the modest blushing kind of young lady we want to experiment upon; will you obey me now, or shall I continue the lesson?"

Julia shrieks and screams: "Ah! Ah! Ah-r-r r re! Oh! Oh! How rude!" the slaps sting more and more, and even her agony cannot prevent her seeing how delighted the Colonel is with his exercise, her bottom seems as if the skin was red-hot, and must burst at every smash; she shrieks and sobs: "Ah! Oh! I shall faint from slaps," which are the best possible remedy for hysteries, &c. At last the agonized girl is compelled to sob out her submission.

The Colonel has experienced the most voluptuous enjoyment from this excitement, he kisses her bottom and still more horrifies the poor girl by other dreadful liberties, at last he advises her to go to bed, and assures her that everything is provided for her comfort, and she need not fear interruption till the "femme de chamber" brings her breakfast in the morning. — "Au revoir, Miss Julia Ponsonby, may I find you obedient and dutiful in every respect tomorrow;" as he takes his exit by the door.

The imprisoned girl passed a restless night, tormented by her apprehension of what was going to happen on the morrow, but towards daylight her exhausted eyes closed in sound sleep, from which she was roughly awakened by someone shaking her naked shoulder, for she had slept in her chemise; to her horror the dreadful Colonel stood by her bedside in his shirt sleeves, one hand grasping a bunch of twigs elegantly tied up with scarlet silk, and velvet round the handle. "Pleasant dreams to you, Miss Julia, you see I have such a fatherly solicitude as to your behaviour before the Aristocratic Flagellants to day, that I am here before breakfast to assure myself that you are in a properly obedient frame of mind," said the dreadful man. "Now get out of bed and dress yourself."

Julia, with blushes and terrified looks, quite delightful to her tormentor. "Oh! Oh! Never before you, this is worse and worse!" Hiding her face under the bed-clothes.

With a sudden wrench the coverlet, blankets, and everything are jerked off her, and she finds herself exposed to his searching gaze in a half-naked state.

Colonel. — "What a beautiful figure, I wonder, Miss Ponsonby, you are not ashamed of going to bed, without proper night dress; but there, it's the old story, females young or old have no sense of decency when they are alone, why I should fear the walls had eyes!"

Distressed and ashamed beyond measure, by his cutting remarks and the sense of shameful exposure, Julia tried to cover herself with a sheet, but a clever switch of his birch, caught her just on the tender parts inside her thighs, and made her quite spring up with the sudden smart, screaming: "Ah! Ah! Oh! Oh! What shall I do!"

Colonel. — "Dress.... Dress.... Dress yourself" as he skilfully cuts her with painfully stinging whisks, which smart more than they do real damage.

At last she is on the floor, the Colonel drops his rod, and picking up her drawers, persists in holding them for her to step into; he is so awkward and makes so many wilful blunders, that poor Julia is ready to die with shame, as he tucks in the tail of her chemise for her, observing: "I shall get more handy bye and bye, I never acted as a ladies' maid before."

The drawers are on at last, and he resumes his rod ordering her to put on her boots and stockings, which operation he watches with gloating satisfaction, as he makes occasional remarks as to the beauty and perfection of her limbs, feeling her calves, nipping her thighs, &c., and otherwise enjoying the distress and shame-faced confusion of his tearful victim. Then he steps back and contemplates her at a short distance, and finally pointing to a ladder standing against the wall, which has somehow mysteriously come into the apartment during her sleep, he orders her slowly to step up three or four rings with her bottom well inclined outwards.

"Stop! High enough!" he shouts out, making his birch hiss through the air as if about to use it. "Now open your drawers behind yourself, and show me your beautiful bottom".... There is a slight hesitation on the part of the victim, but the rod instantly slashes down on her covered buttocks with such force, that she gives a fearful scream of agony, and falls off the ladder, writhing on the ground and rubbing her bottom as she sobs: "Oh! Oh! Oh! Oh!"

He seizes her by the hair of her head and fairly lifts her on to her feet, threatening that he will take her life and get some other girl, if she does not promise to obey his most trifling, or most painful orders, without regard to her own feelings of pain.

"I will torture you slowly to death, silly obstinate girl," he hissed in her ear.

Julia thought her last hour had really come, she screamed: "Mercy! Mercy! Mercy! Oh! I will do anything, Sir! Oh! Oh!"

Satisfied with the effects of his threats, he contented himself by making the terribly humiliated girl stand on her head against the wall, with the slit of her drawers so open that he could see the slightly pouting lips of her cunny surrounded by a light chevelure of hair almost as golden as that streaming from her head to the floor.

At length he left her with strict injunctions to dress herself as if for a ball, assuring her that the best way to secure his approbation would be to attend to his directions in that respect, adding that Mary would furnish her with an elegant change in place of the damaged dress she had on yesterday.

THE LECTURE

The Aristocratic Flagellants, after a sumptuous dinner, (from which even the ladies rose slightly flushed by the champagne they had indulged in) adjourned for the evening's entertainment to their Paradise as they styled the beautiful conservatory, having an unshaken faith between themselves that Adam and Eve re-invigorated one another by slapping each others' bottoms, in the original garden of Eden, where, of course their only pleasure was a luscious indulgence in all the arts of love, nowadays condemned by a hypocritical world as wicked and obscene, but which in those primeval times formed the true end and object of harmless lives continually striving to obey their maker's first and greatest commandment to "Multiply and replenish the earth."

The Colonel had left the table some quarter of an hour in advance of the company, begging they would excuse him as he was only going to enquire after Miss Julia's health, and would himself introduce her to them in Paradise.

Repairing to the victim's room he found the young lady dressed in an elegant ball costume of dark blue silk, trimmed with honey-lace, which contrasted in a most fascinating manner with her lovely blonde complexion, the golden hair hanging in a profusion of ringlets over her finely moulded shoulders, which were fully exposed, and a close observer could see the upper part of the ivory globes of her bosom, as they heaved with tumultuous agitation under the thin shading of lace.

"Excuse my intrusion, Miss Ponsonby," said the Colonel, with rigid politeness, "I see you have paid attention to your toilette, but by St. Bridget, you look as obstinate as ever with your tear-stained face; how is it, girl? For we are going to meet all the ladies and gentlemen directly. Are you going to smile or not?" as he flourished a sharp cutting ladies-riding whip before the terrified girl.

Julia. — "Indeed, sir, I have paid attention to your instructions, and hope Mary has dressed me to your satisfaction, but it's quite impossible for me not to show my fear and anxiety," standing up and looking at him with her splendid large eyes red and brimful of tears.

Colonel. — "Wipe your eyes directly, Miss Ponsonby, this is real childishness; I must make you look cheerful, if not delighted," slashing her with his little whip over her arms and shoulders, the delicate skin of which instantly showed deep red marks.

Julia, the tears running down her crimson cheeks, and the corners of her mouth twisting up as she suppresses her cries, only sobs, but dashes away from his reach, wringing her hands in agony.

Her tormentor follows her up — Slash! slash!! slash!!! — The room is too small for her to evade his blows, which whirl through the air and seem to cut the poor girl like a knife, raising a number of hot smarting weals, one or two of which are on her burning face.

Colonel. — "I'll cut you to pieces. There's only a few minutes before I must introduce you, and now you are making yourself quite unpresentable," getting more and more excited.

She darts about the room shrieking frantically: "Mercy! Mercy! Mercy! Oh! Oh! Oh! Ah-r-r-re!" as she stumbled over a footstool and nearly fainted away.

Colonel. — "Ha! Ha! I think you begin to know me a little; if it was not for spoiling your appearance, you would not get off so easily, Miss Julia; now let Mary help you to compose yourself," as the "femme de chamber" appears in answer to his summons.

Julia takes a little of a most exhilarating cordial, which seems to make her feel quite gay in an instant; still the marks of her whipping tell a painful tale, even after her eyes and face have been carefully washed with Eau de Cologne; the Colonel also was glad of a few minutes rest to compose his own excited feelings.

The company were getting slightly impatient when the Colonel entered the conservatory with Julia upon his arm.

They all rose and inclined themselves gracefully towards their victim as their president presented her saying: "This is Miss Julia Ponsonby, well-known to most of you; and I trust we shall all enjoy the most delicious sensations as, by her aid, I am able to illustrate the theory of discipline; unfortunately she has required some considerable drilling with this little tickler to get her into something like an approach to a proper state of submissiveness."

Julia is so bewildered at the sight of six ladies in masks, and four gentlemen made up with most ferocious false whiskers and moustaches, that she fails to bow to them in return, but, dropping the arm of her introducer, retreats to the further end of the place close to the fountain, crying hysterically, her face, neck, and little white hands showing the marks of the cruel cuts she had received.

The ladies on their part are quite in a flutter, and, masked as they are, can feel their faces tingling with a kind of reticent shame, as they find themselves in the presence of their victim, a young lady they have been accustomed to meet at all the best houses of the aristocracy; and what were they about to do to her? The thought of all the indignities and shameful insults they should see perpetrated on the beautiful modest young girl made their blood thrill with impulsive rushes of excited anticipations; the Colonel is the only one who fairly shows his natural features, the ladies have their masks: Lady Manvers (blue), Lady Curzon (red), Miss Debrette (black), Hon. Miss Cuddleton (yellow), whilst the gentlemen: Sir Charles Dansy, Captain Cooper, Lord Flashington, and the Marquis of Crim-Con, are known respectively as red, brown, black, and blue beards.

All are impatient for the lecturer to commence, and the Colonel throwing down the whip which he had retained in his right hand: "There is my young beauty that will lie on the floor to remind you of the warning you have had; no wonder you have retreated close to the cool fountain! Stand in the middle of the room! Do you hear me, Miss?" he almost thundered, stamping with his foot to make his impatience more terrible to the victim.

Convulsively sobbing and wringing her smarting hands, Miss Ponsonby takes her stand as ordered and the Colonel proceeds: "Now, ladies, I want you to follow me in my lecture both in its practical and well as its theoretical bearings, and I promise you a treat, but first let me observe that in the case of a young lady, such as the subject before you, it would have been impossible for me to collect my ideas with sufficient clearness and composure unless I had just cowed her proud spirit: An aristocratic young lady is like an untamed filly from the steppes of Tartary or the rolling prairie. She may be modest and retiring in ordinary, but the moment she feels the curb of strict obedience forced upon her, she feels insulted, degraded, and decidedly restive; the only effective plan in such a case is to assume a savage relentless manner, and use plenty of whip as I have done at the very beginning; it cowes their spirit quicker than anything. I have explained to Miss Ponsonby that she will have to obey the minutest orders I may give, even to strip naked and ask me if such and such a charm is not pretty, if we should not like to feel it, or examine it to please ourselves. I've thrashed her shrieking round that room, and only desisted on her promising the most implicit obedience; and again I told her giving slash after slash just now, that what I meant by obedience was stripping herself when ordered to do so, slowly, one thing at a time, till by a very gradual process she might even be stark naked; and now let me ask you all to come close and examine her marks, her blushes, tears, and quivering lips; imagine all the pain she has already suffered before I could bring her into this half-trained state, for I am sure she will be restive again; but that will only tend to make this lecture more piquant. It makes our pleasure the greater; that was a painful cut (touching one); bend your neck, Miss, so that the ladies can see where the marks are."

The poor girl is more crimson than ever, she bites her lips till the blood comes, as she tries to repress her indignant feelings; they can see how deeply she feels it all; and the gentlemen amuse themselves by placing their hand on her palpitating bosom, and drawing their female friends' attention to her agitated condition.

Lady Manvers, with a flutter of mixed excitement and sympathy: "Poor child, I would kiss and soothe you but for this horrid blue domino; you have cut her about, sir! Augh! what a nasty cut that is! I don't think I like such cruelty; but still it's very exciting to see a man flogging a lady," as she pats the poor crimson girl caressingly: "Poor thing, I won't be one to see you punished so severely."

Julia. — "Oh! Oh! Don't touch me! Ah-r-r-re! Oh! Dear Lady, you seem to have some kind feeling; let me go; make them give me my liberty. Oh! Oh! what have I done to deserve such punishment? Oh! I can't bear it!" wringing her hands in agony and more distressed than ever.

Miss Debrette. — "Don't be so soft-hearted, she can bear it well enough. I've seen a pretty good lot of birching in my time, and it was always an exquisite sight to see the girls' bottoms exposed! My schoolmistress was quite delighted when once I saw her place three sisters side by side with their clothes turned up and dunces' caps on their heads; she did cut them up, all three at once; our blood was so delightfully heated by the sight that three of us slipped away for a little amusement afterwards; but perhaps you, Lady Blue, don't understand that sort of thing, if so, it will be improper to enlighten you, especially as Miss Ponsonby might hear it; There! there! just look at her, how I have made her blushes deepen; why I think the lewd young lady quite understands what I refer to."

Julia is all confusion, as she once had a bedfellow who secretly taught her some curious, but very pleasing practices.

Colonel, giving the victim a rather loud sounding slap on her sore neck, which elicits quite a sudden scream of pain: "I think you are quite right in your conjecture, Miss Black, or she would never have blushed as she does, she shall confess it all bye and bye, and perhaps you can tell us something amusing when I feel to require a few moments' rest during my lecture?" Then his heavy hand gives a couple more pitiful slaps, as poor Julia screams in agony: "Ah! Ah-r-r-re! Oh: How cruel!" then he continues: "Cruelty! Nonsense! Why, you don't know what it is yet! you'll soon give over that idea..... Stand straight, or I'll take up the whip again..... Stand up! so!" as he pretends to be looking for the dreaded whip.

"Now to go on with my lecture," he continues, "there is whipping fantastic, and there is whipping in earnest. These are used by persons of various temperaments, or like myself they vary their punishments so as to thoroughly enjoy all the voluptuous ideas they can possibly raise by watching the varied contortions and studying all the feelings of their victims as each kind of humiliation or downright torture is brought into play."

"I may describe the fantastic whipping as when a true lover of the rod first makes his victim kiss the rod and asks her flagellator to punish her properly as he knows it is for her goods; then she has to strip herself gradually, removing first her dress, and then her petticoats, one by one, whilst he perhaps kneels down and examines her pretty feet, calves, and thighs, his nippings and touches putting her into an indescribable flutter of shame as her modesty is shocked more and more every moment; this with a fresh victim who is quite unprepared for what is going to happen affords a fine treat to all the spectators, as they watch the tears of shame streaming down her crimson cheeks whilst the burning blushes may be seen to cross her indignant face in deeper flushes every moment. And then generally there is a little restiveness to be subdued till at last the young lady stands with nothing to hide all the charms of her lovely person, but her thin chemise, and a deliciously pretty pair of elegantly trimmed drawers; having got your palpitating modest young beauty into this state, you must order her to turn round so that you may admire her figure from behind, then make with her own hands open the slit of her drawers and expose her own snow-bottom for your admiration; pat it, slap it, make each blow sound well through the apartment, perhaps she will shriek under the smarting impact of your hands on her tender flesh, but that only adds music to your entertainment, encourage her to cry out well, as it will do her good; make laughing and jeering remarks about her buttocks, how rosy, red, or peach-like they look, make her look at her own bottom in a glass, show her the reflection of her own shamed and indignant looks, enjoy her humiliation in every possible way. Next we come to the horse, the one you see before you is a real Berkeley, with a ladder arrangement added to it. Besides that convenient article for arranging our subject in almost every attitude we might wish to see her, we have a gibbet twelve feet high which a couple of gentlemen could put up in the centre of this place in less than five minutes. It is fitted with hooks, ropes and pulleys. We can treat Miss Julia Ponsonby here, to a nice little swing, or if the fancy takes us suspend her head downwards to receive part of practical illustrations to this lecture."

"Yet this is to be a practical as well as theoretical

lecture. I quite fancy Miss Julia is getting impatient of my discourse. I would almost rather face the reality, but before we begin, I wish to explain how it is that ladies so much enjoy seeing a modest girl abashed and mortified by being unwillingly exposed."

"Not one of you, ladies, happening to go into the Parks to enjoy the sights of skating, sliding, and all the various amusements going on, but you fully expect to see one of your fair sex make some unwilling display of herself by slipping or falling so as to expose her legs, thighs, or better still a pretty bottom; such a sight makes you blush, but inwardly a warm exciting thrill passes through your veins in the feverish hope of another such accident happening. The other day I saw a beautiful girl suddenly unhorsed as she was riding in the park, and for a moment her foot was entangled in the stirrup or something of the sort, making a most luscious display of all her charms, a bevy of ladies a few paces behind the unfortunate equestrienne blushed crimson at the sight but I could see their eyes sparkle with unwonted animation, whilst I overheard one fair lady remark to her husband: "What a bottom for to slap," in imitation of old Blucher's exclamation about London as he gazed on our rich and gorgeous shops: "Vat a zity fur to sack," and I was of the same opinion, as my hand mechanically gave a flourishing cut with my whip, making my horse almost plunge over the prostrate beauty, she deserved a whipping for falling off and exposing herself so. All ladies, however ashamed they may look, are inwardly delighted to witness any little accident of the sort, such as when a young lady's dress gets blown over her head, the very idea of knowing how distressing it is to the sufferer enhances their pleasure."

"Now, Miss Ponsonby, let me recommend your

obedience, or —" flourishing the whip significantly, "you will know what is coming ... Kneel down!"

Julia, screaming: — "Oh! Oh! Oh! What are you going to do? I can't! Oh! It's so dreadful! I'm so frightened! ... Ah-r-r-r-re! I will!" as he begins to slash the whip across her shoulders.

Colonel. — "Wait a moment, I have a few more observations to make, after you have secured your victim to the ladder, say, with her hands stretched high above her head, secured by the wrists high up, then her legs being also secured by the ankles to rings at the post, and the ladder being wider at the bottom than higher up, her legs are well apart. Birch in hand, the operator begins to lecture the victim upon her intractable disposition, her haughty proud spirit or anything else that comes to his mind as suitable for the occasion, but of course it is best when the young lady has to be punished for some special fault."

"Open her drawers behind, and put aside the tail of her chemise, so as to give a good view of her pretty bottom, pin back her drawers or pull them down to her knees whichever you prefer; the sight of a really modest young lady when first tied up to the ladder is a most exquisite treat, watch her flashing indignant eyes, and also perhaps she will break out into passionate appeals or reproaches, as anxiety or indignation may have the uppermost place in her mind at the moment, all this you have to enjoy and turn to advantage; study the blushing waves which cross her tear-stained face, and suffuse their warm tints over both neck and bosom. I have even seen the young innocent bottoms change colour when first exposed to public view. Be very deliberate in all you do; continually ask her how she likes it, if she is disposed to be more obedient, if she is sorry for her faults, &c., touching her up from time to time by smart stinging applications of the green switch-tail, make her scream, writhe and wince under your skilful whisks of the rod; suddenly a smarter cut than usual right up under the crack of her bottom will make the plunging restive beauty cry out in terrible agony: "Ah! Ha! Ha!" You like that better, Miss Rosy Bum? There another! And another! As you give a couple more, making the tips of the pliant birch search out even the lips of her tender charms."

"All this is exquisitely agonizing to the poor victim; and the shocks to her modesty cause even more painful sensations than the keenest cuts you can give; she feels the depths of her degradation, and is intensely humiliated at the thought of these cruel cuts being given in the presence of her own sex as spectators, and the men are laughing, jeering, and enjoying all her cries and every motion. All I can say is keep up the game, vary the flagellation by using whips, holly or nettles; if she faints revive her again, and make her last as long as possible."

"Now I may go on with the practical part once more. Miss Ponsonby, you've had a little respite, kiss the rod and stand up," said the Colonel presenting the birch to her quivering lips.

Julia kisses the birch, with a sob which seems to come from the bottom of her heart; it was so deep and impressive. She looks round appealing as in hopes someone may pity her, but only meets the sparkling eyes behind the dominoes of the ladies, which plainly attest the excitement of their owners, whilst the bearded gentlemen are gloating over her agony, remarking to one another: "Look at the darling; how beautifully she blushes, how would our ladies like it themselves; see, see; Miss Black is quite agitated by her excitement!" Then old Blue Beard ejaculates: "By Heaven! I couldn't spare her if she was my own child! In fact it would make it more exquisite," rubbing his hands and in his excitement giving the Honourable Miss in the yellow domino a most impudent pinch behind, which that spirited young lady resents by a sharp slap on the face making his ears tingle, which affords great amusement to the others.

Colonel (calmly). "Very well.... Now, Miss Ponsonby, Julia, I should say; I'm going to ask you to expose your limbs. Of course it's very unpleasant for a young lady of your age and brought up as you have been, to do such a thing; I know you will think it immodest, disgusting, shocking, and awfully degrading, but I am about to illustrate my lecture, and the more humiliated we can make the expression of your pretty blushing face, the more enjoyable will be the tableau, I want my friends here to thoroughly appreciate.... Ah! You tremble.... Don't hide your face in your hands.... It spoils my picture.... Look straight at me and tell me, if you have drawers, on Julia? Eh? I presume it is so... Answer me!"

A deeper scarlet flush mantles over the beautiful features of the unhappy girl, as with another choking sob, she nods her head and instantly buries her burning face again her hands.

Colonel (sharply): "Don't nod! Answer! And take your hands away from your face!"

Julia. — "Ye-e-e-es," trembling from head to foot in her great agitation.

Colonel. "Now I dare say, ladies, you wonder why I asked that question. I will tell you; a gradually slow process of disrobing is much more exciting to me as it will be to you. Each article is removed one at the time till the last skirt, when, if she had no drawers the sudden exposure of all her delicious charms at once would rather spoil the effect, where as if a young lady has drawers on, we make her open them for us, and show us a little of her bottom, explain the use of the slit in front, &c. You will find this awfully voluptuous in the curious sensations you will feel as Miss Julia has to do all this before your delighted eyes; you must see the looks, thoroughly enjoy them, and appreciate all her mental sufferings. Long before you can see, you will be picturing to yourselves the beauties that are still to be exposed, you will have a loveable yearning towards your victim, and yet long to humiliate her and shock her modesty still more. It seems to me that the mixture of these opposite sentiments causes the exquisite thrills which rush through our veins. It is indeed the sublimity of Flagellation, and I cannot but assure you that in Buckle's Tracts which are so usually considered the masterpiece of an expert is nothing to be compared to the experience you will have this evening; Coleman's *Rodiad* is better as more spirited, but his victim was a rough vulgar workhouse boy, and so it's as the difference between barbarism and civilisation; give me Miss Julia here, a modest, virtuous, and well educated young lady, who will shudder and blush at every order she compelled to obey."

Here a clapping of hands all round assured the speaker of their unqualified applause.

Colonel, (resuming): "I understand you appreciate my remarks. I know I am far from eloquent, but such a delightful subject warms us all. Perhaps it is best not to make her remove all her petticoats but order her to raise them for us to examine and handle (I hope they won't pinch the poor girl,) her calves and thighs; if they should be so rude it might make her suddenly drop her skirts, and then, of course, she have to begin again, and prolong her confusion and distress. Did I hear someone say; "Begin! Begin!" I will only remark that we shall at last get those pretty drawers off altogether, and your excited expectations will be fully gratified."

Poor Julia was a sight both to pity and to admire, her eyes flashing with indignation at Colonel's glowing eulogy on his process of mental degradation, by making her slowly expose herself, and then tears of fear and shame as she felt her helpless and hopeless situation, the prolonged agony was simply inexpressible.

Colonel. — "We're now going into the practical illustration of what I have been saying; look well at Miss Ponsonby, study her emotions. Fancy yourselves before a strange gentleman, pulling up your drawers, letting them down and so on, your disgust at the rude handling, and remarks on the beauty of your calves, the firm plumpness of the ivory thighs, &c. — and then — Ah! Ah! Oh! Oh! you shriek from some sly pinch or unexpectedly rude advance, you must keep all these things in mind to appreciate my lecture."

Then turning to his trembling victim who has been so awfully shocked and abashed, that she stands before him with burning face, and her eyes closed to save her the pain of seeing the excited glares of her persecutors, he proceeds:

"Now, Julia, look up again!... So.... Now take the whole of your petticoats up to your knees, look the company full in the face, and see how they feel and sympathise with your sufferings, now begin slowly!... Ah! You won't?... Ha! I thought you would think better of it!"

He had given her a sharp awakener with his birch across the tender skin of her shoulders, making the part look quite bruised with its fiery red marks. Julia does not actually scream, but the flowing tears and the twitching of her mouth show what painful effort it costs her to restrain her cries, her nervous fingers clutch her skirts and raise them with a sudden jerk.

The black-bearded gentleman drops on his knees and handles the beautiful legs, exclaiming in rapturous excitement: "What a lovely pair of calves! What pretty stockings and boots!" passing his hand up and down from the ankles to the knees. Then again: "Your garter is unbuckled, will you allow me to put it right, dear Miss Ponsonby?" as he purposely bungles so as to feel her soft firm flesh under her drawers.

This is too much, the indignant Julia restively spurns him with her delicate feet, so forcibly as almost to overturn his lordship, who turns pale with anger, as he sees how amused the others are at his discomfiture.

Colonel (interposing): "Gently, my Lord! Allow me to make her properly obedient," as he picks up the dreadful little whip and lays aside the birch rod; then turning upon poor Julia, who is already frightened at what she has done in her impetuosity, gives her a couple of most painful cuts on the ankles which are exposed by the partly raised skirts. "Now, you hot tempered young lady, let me remind you that such pretty little feet were never made to kick with, only brutal men are allowed to do such vulgar things. Fie! Fie! Miss Ponsonby where are your good manners?"

Julia almost drops with the sudden pain of these blows and cannot repress her shrieks this time, each cut eliciting a heart piercing scream of "Ah-r-r-re! Oh! Oh! Ah-r-r-re!" as she wrings her hands in agony.

Colonel. — "Now, Miss Julia, ask the gentleman with the black beard for his pardon and express your regret at being so hasty."

Julia. — "Yes! Oh! Yes! I am sorry, Sir,...... pray, forgive that nasty kick......," then seeing the whip about to descend upon her shoulders, she screams: "Oh! Oh! Pray, don't strike me! I will! I will! I'll bear anything!"

Mr. Black-beard. — "Poor girl, you did make me very angry, but I do forgive you now, as all I did was in great sympathy for your wounded and humiliated feelings."

Colonel (sternly): "Now, Julia, you had better remove your dress and outer petticoats, leaving only your fine white underskirt to lift; take them off one by one, and mind, look as pleased as you can."

The poor girl is in a dreadful state of apprehension, her hands tremble so, she can scarcely help herself as she tries to divest herself of her dress, and old Blue-beard hastens to help her, laughing: "Ha! Ha! Ha! I've done for a lady's maid before now. I'm sure dear Miss Julia will be glad of a little assistance; that nasty whip and his lordship's blundering rudeness have quite unnerved her." The victim instinctively shrinks from his touch as she knows it is only to increase her shame and humiliation; what hot burning blushes suffuse her tear-stained face as she feels his hand roving over her neck and bosom in pretended officiousness; the marquis is delighted with his self-imposed task, calling the attention of ladies and gentlemen to the throbbing globes of Julia's bosom. "Look, did you ever see a sweeter bust; what a downy pillow for your lover's head, my dear," as he pinches the little strawberry nipples quite painfully, till fresh tears roll down her distressed cheeks, and deep sighs attest the depth of her exquisite agony and shame.

Then by a spasmodic effort she gets rid of her next two underskirts, and stands a picture of grief and shame, in white petticoats and drawers, which fit tightly to her figure.

Colonel (who is greatly excited at the sight): "Now, be careful, not too quick; just lift your petticoat, Julia, as high as the middle of your thigh, and allow Mr. Black-beard to resume his examination; I believe he will marry you if he approves of all your charms, and I can assure you, he would be a good match."

Julia is in such confusion, that she slightly hesitates before lifting her skirt, but the relentless whip cuts her pretty plump arms till she shrieks in agony and is really unable to hold anything, wringing her hands and sobbing: "Oh! Oh! Oh! How cruel! I will! I will!"

Colonel (getting still more excited and seeing that his audience are almost in the same state): "Will you mind what I say in future, and not let that obstinate proud spirit of yours so continually show itself; eh, Miss? Must I be so cruel? Is it not your own stupid hesitation which drives me to it?" slashing away over her shoulder, neck and arms, till Julia, giving a prolonged cry of agony falls to the floor and they find she has fainted.

All the excited ladies and gentlemen crowd round their victim. The lady in the blue-domino is really most tender-hearted and sympathetic, she lays the poor girl's head in her lap, chafes her hands with strong aromatic vinegar, puts pungent salts to her nostrils, and as soon as there is the faintest sign of returning animation, pours some most invigorating cordial down Julia's parched throat, which has such a wonderful effect that in less than ten minutes she is standing stronger than ever before the Colonel.

Her swollen eyes run over with hot scalding tears which trickle over her burning cheeks, her tongue almost cleaves to the roof of her mouth, but the cordial gives her strength to a make a pitiful appeal. Extending her arms, which are scored with raw looking weals, and slightly blood-stained in places, she sobs out: "Have you no pity, ladies? Are your hearts as cruel as these gentlemen's? Look at these cuts and bruises. Ah! Ah! Oh! Oh! What pleasure can you find in this torture?" as she sees their sparkling eyes all glow with extraordinary vivacity.

Colonel. — "I'm sure they all feel for you, we all do, as I said before the mixture of sympathy and excitement is deliciously voluptuous; now lift your skirt nearly up to your bottom, Mr. Black-beard is excitedly anxious to go on with his investigations, he thinks as the French do that every lover ought to be perfectly assured of all the charms of his inamorats before marriage, and begged me to procure a suitable young lady, whom he could examine in our presence."

Julia, looking down in confusion, and not daring

to disobey the order, lifts up the skirt as high as the middle of her thighs, sobbing out at the same time: "Oh! Sir, have mercy, I don't want to be married. Oh! Oh! Oh! I could not help it. Oh! not to him, no. Oh! Oh! Forgive me, Sir," as the whip cuts round her thighs a little above the knee, raising the marks even under the drawers, which fit tightly on the plump, well rounded contour of her figure from the hips downwards; the poor girl fairly writhes and twists in agony, and goes on sobbing hysterically: "Oh! Oh! Oh!"

Colonel. — "That was to make you more polite to your lover in future; really, Julia, I think you have lost all your good and polite manners somewhere, at least you don't show them here; now, as a special penance, pull up your drawers so as the gentleman may see the painful bruises on your white thighs." The drawers are pulled up as far as her plump thighs will allow.

Julia. — "Oh! Sir, pray, don't touch me again, the contact of your fingers...." Here she breaks down, as she feels his hands feeling and pinching the flesh with a kind of savage pleasure.

Colonel (with a savage groan): "What were you going to say, speak out, I hope it was nothing to hurt his Lordship's sensitiveness again. What was it, Julia?" making his whip this time cut the naked skin so that little drops of blood ooze from the abraded part.

Julia (in intense pain): "Mercy! Mercy!! I'll submit to anything, if only you spare me, my flesh is so tender, every cut will draw the blood. Oh! Heavens! What an accumulation of fearful shame and pain!" She goes on sobbing while the tears roll continually down her crimson face.

Colonel (delighted at the effect of his cuts): "So you have such a thin delicate skin, Miss Julia, then you will feel the cuts more acutely; if your bottom is as tender as your thighs we shall have an exquisite treat presently; now, turn your back to me and open your drawers behind, and mind you ask the gentleman who is so attentively solicitous about you, to put his hand kindly inside and pull up the tail of your chemise for you, whilst you hold them open for us all to have a good view."

All this the trembling victim has to submit to, but the Colonel and his company thoroughly enjoy all the looks of disgust and bitter shame, which pass in rapid succession over her distressed features, more especially when the gentleman's hand in searching for the tail end of her chemise, makes her feel all sorts of indignities as it invades her most private parts; the chemise pulled up, they can see that Julia's bottom, although beautifully shaped and plump, is quite refined in its proportions, the skin white and delicate with pretty looking dimples all over it, and every touch of the gentleman's hand seems to bring up a slight rosy tint as he exclaims in ecstasy to the Colonel: "What a duck of a bottom, no wonder there are cannibals in the world, any one could eat such delicate flesh as that," giving a loving bite on one cheek of the victim's buttocks, which makes her scream again with pain, and feel the most intense mortification.

Colonel. — "How pretty your teeth-marks look in her flesh, if I had had a bite, there would have been a piece out," then gives the other cheek of her bottom a couple of light lively cuts, which leave long red marks and make the surface blush all over, as he says: "There! There!! They're a couple of smarters just to make you forget about his teeth; pay attention; pull your drawers more open; now walk round the company two or three times, keeping them well open as they are. March! March!! March!!!" Giving light smarting cuts at each word to her on the move: "Look, ladies," he continues, "how beautifully her skin flushes under even these light touches of the whip; now, Julia, do you thoroughly feel your humiliation, do you feel the uttermost possible shame?"

At this last cruel question the poor girl quite breaks down, crying, and between her tears sobbing out hysterically: "Ah, Sir! How am I to bear all this? For mercy's sake let me die... Put an end to this torture," and then giving vent to her pent up feelings, she shrieks: "Mercy! Mercy!! Have you not a particle of pity in your cruel hearts?"

Here the Colonel, who is delighted at the state of mental agony in which he has thrown his victim, goes up to her, and whispers in her ear that the lady in the blue domino is the only one who has a little softness in her dispositions: "Ask her, poor Julia, if she does not indeed pity you?"

Julia. — "Oh! Madame, can you see all this without pity for the poor victim?" casting her eyes with a most pitiful look towards the blue domino.

Lady. — "Well, to say the truth, I really do, poor girl, but, at the same time, it all excites me so that I really revel in your shame and humiliation; turn round, child; open your drawers as wide as possible.... What a lovely bottom!"

Colonel (slightly pricking her buttocks with a pin to test the delicacy of the fair skin): "See, the least touch brings the ruby virgin blood to the surface; now, Julia, have the goodness to unfasten your drawers!... You'd better obey quickly, Miss... That's right... Now push them down to feet... Do you hear?"

The victim is fairly dazed with shame and confusion: the Colonel whispers in her ear that she must slap herself well; then saying loudly: "Do it slowly so that each slap may be distinctly heard: Harder! Harder! Make them sound better, my girl, it's a most amusing and exciting sight to see a young lady slapping herself, and exposing her beautiful person in such a variety of ways; all your motions are graceful; each incident of your degradation is most voluptuously interesting to every one of us. Now, Miss Ponsonby, I can see his lordship is getting quite excited at the rude exhibition you're making of yourself, and no doubt it has been most irksome and shamefully degrading to your feelings you must oblige him now with a full view of your virgin charms; here rest yourself in the president's easy chair, kick off your drawers, that's it, sit down and rest yourself..... Pull up your chemise to your waist..... Just so, now one leg over each arm of the chair, so that I may fully dilate upon all your charms to his lordship, who intends to marry you at the close of my lecture..... He has arranged for a most respectable clergyman to attend when called for, and has special license from His Grace the Archbishop of Canterbury."

Julia is quite overwhelmed at this compulsory exhibition of herself, but is slightly comforted to think that by being married her disgrace and shame will be covered, however she may dislike her bridegroom. Still this last degradation cuts her modesty to the quick, although she is so afraid of the whip as to submit as quietly as possible.

Colonel (continuing): "now we have a model of virtuous

immodesty. Miss Julia, I would give 1000 P.st. to have that position of yours preserved in coloured marble with all your shame and indignation truly depicted in your face as we see it at this moment, but to go on, let me point out all your beauties to your intended husband: My Lord, in the first place notice the pretty light curly hair which adorns her prominent mons veneris, look at the vermillion lips which her position has caused to open slightly in a most inviting manner. Ha! Ha!! She little imagines what a luscious sight she presents to your view; then, you observe that little knob of flesh hiding its head between them, what do you call it, Julia? Eh! You don't know, my demure young lady," giving it a painful little cut.

Julia (with a painful shriek): "Oh! Oh! Ah-r-r-r-r-re! Spare me! Oh! How can I say what I don't know?"

Colonel (with a most delightful look all round): "How funny that ladies generally don't know the name of the most amorous little bit of themselves; well, Julia, it's called the clitoris, and is a most excitable little affair; bye the bye, I remember your confusion at first, did you never have it touched by a bedfellow? It was something said by the lady in the blue domino which seemed to disconcert you, now I must know all about it, speak up; look me straight in the face."

Julia. — "Oh! Oh!! To be compelled to speak of such a thing; it was one of the governesses got me to sleep with her, and then she tickled me so there that.... That...." Here she breaks down overpowered by the sense of her burning shame, covering her face with both hands as well as with her chemise, and again sobbing as if her heart would break, thus unconsciously making a still more ravishing exposure of her beautiful snow-white belly.

Colonel. — "Come, come; it's nothing so bad after all: now, how did she make you feel? Speak up or the whip shall make you," giving a slight switch across the navel which leaves its cruel mark on her delicate skin.

Julia. — "Indeed... Indeed, I never trusted myself with her again, she made the blood so hot in my veins that I seemed to blush all over, and at last... at last... Oh! Oh! Don't ask me any more," she sobs again hiding her crimson face in her chemise.

Colonel (his whole frame quivering with delighted excitement): "Well now, Miss, you're making a beautifully lewd exposure of yourself, can't you tell us what the "at last" was?"

Julia. — "Ah! Oh! I couldn't help it, but I .. I .. don't know... I .. I .. was all wet," this was gasped out with a terribly distressing effort.

Colonel. — "Ha! Ha! Ha! You innocent child, that is what most ladies call "coming or spending," I think the rest of the company quite understand it; look, Julia, see how your exhibition has excited them."

The fact was three of the gentlemen had dragged Miss Debrette (black domino) and stretched her on the horse, turned up her skirts and displayed a lovely pair of drawers and legs, and they were in the act of opening her drawers behind, their victim as themselves kicking, plunging and shrieking for mercy.

The Colonel takes Julia by the hand and they all crowd round to see the fun; the victim being a very dark lady her exposed rump formed quite a contrast to that of Miss Ponsonby, she was of Spanish extraction and had a slightly olive tint as complexion of her skin.

The Captain as he pulled her drawers fairly open, exclaiming in delight: "Now, Miss Ponsonby, you can enter into the fun of the thing; I think Colonel that Miss Julia ought to handle the twigs, and repay on this lady's posteriors some of the indignities she has herself had to feel."

Julia. — "Oh! Pray excuse me, I'm neither cruel or revengeful, it's so indelicate," turning down her eyes, and blushing at the sight.

Colonel. — "The Captain has made a most proper suggestion, you must take the birch in hand, Julia, whilst I will whisper in your ear how to apply it, so that we shall soon see if the blood of the Spanish Dons is better than our own blue strain." Then producing a very fine tight fitting pair of drawers, the gentlemen assist the blushing agitated girl to put them on, his lordship taking care to arrange her comfortably inside with his hands, till Julia quite sobs for shame at his prolonged attentions.

Captain. — "What a pretty effect tight fitting drawers give to a modest young lady: they leave so much to the imagination, which acts as a stimulant to our excitement, the unseen invariably has a certain fascination, it is the greatest peculiarity of human nature, that we always desire forbidden fruit, and the ladies so thoroughly appreciate the weakness in men that they know the surest way to excite love or admiration is to hide all, or at least the tenderest charms from sight, leaving us, as we watch their graceful motions, to burn with feverish desire as our heated imaginations picture every thing in the loveliest possible colour. Heaven grant the day may never come when female beauty is fully exposed to view, the very surfeit as well as the sameness of the charms would pall upon our senses and render us indifferent; I consider the man who wrote "Beauty unadorned is adorned the most" was a fool and could not possibly have estimated the effect of a world full of naked unblushing females, where could we then look for the timid modesty which suffuses the maiden's cheek with a flush of shame, every thing would be rude, and rough, and vulgar, to say nothing of the loss of delicate complexions, always so lovely to look upon, when we occasionally get a real Venus unveiled."

Colonel. — "I quite agree with you, but it is not only the gentlemen but the ladies also who would regret such a return to barbarism, they derive such exquisite pleasure in seeing the accidental humiliation of one of their own sex before a number of laughing men and boys, there is a secret voluptuous feeling which they do not even admit themselves, their acute and sensitive imaginations make them enjoy mortification, distress, and feeling of smallness, which they know the unfortunate lady must feel as she frantically struggles to arrange her disordered garments, and retreats from the scene of her discomfiture with scarlet face and a feeling of wanting to sink into the ground. You have all had it illustrated in the case of Miss Ponsonby this evening, you have seen the innate modesty of a sensitively virtuous young lady shocked in every possible way, and I feel sure have enjoyed the sight of her pain, shame, and awful humiliating sense of degradation, if I said more I should appear too prolix; now, Miss Julia, I expect you to illustrate a little of my theory on the inviting bottom before you," as he hands the blushing hesitating girl a fine large birch rod, elegantly tied and ornamented with blue velvet and red silk ribbons.

Julia takes it with a trembling hand, and flourishes through the air, thinking in her innocence to delay the commencement of her indelicate task, but the Colonel whispers in her ear: "Well done, now bring it down with a good whack right across; now another, and another," and then again he whispers: "Lecture your victim upon something; accuse her of pride, obstinacy, indecency, anything you can call to mind as suitable," adding a most fearful threat which makes the blushing face of Miss Ponsonby turn quite pale for the moment.

Thus urged and threatened, the sense of self preservation impulled the poor girl to try and tease her tormentors, and she soon began to cut away quite willingly. The Colonel was pleased but he took up the whip to frighten Julia into beginning her lecture; she understood his significant hint, and blushing to the very roots of her hair, commenced:—

"I am glad to have this lady in the black domino as my victim, as I think she rightly deserves to feel what pain and mental torture such as I have been through is like: now, Miss, will you beg my pardon for your unkind remarks and the cruel pleasure you evinced at the sight of my sufferings; how do you like that and that!! And that!!!" Warming to her work as she remembers, she is cutting into the bottom of the most cruelly sensual lady in the room.

Victim. — "No, no! Never!! You are such a sensitively modest little chit that I revelled in your shame and mortification; your strokes only recall to me the delicious flood that thrilled through my veins as I enjoyed the intensity of your humiliation."

Julia, prompted by the Colonel, and excited by

this very aggravating reply (for Miss Debrette was so fond of flagellation she delighted in being whipped and excited by the rod till the skin was literally thrashed off her bottom, being after a while quite insensible to pain, and oblivious to everything but the voluptuous emotions she was so fond of experiencing even at the expense of intense preliminary suffering), cuts her most painfully inside the thighs and then right up under the crack of her bottom, so sharply that the blood began to trickle in little streams down the inside of the victim's thighs and into her drawers as they hung about the knees.

Victim. — "Ah! Oh! My God! Have mercy: you'll kill me. Oh! To think of such a modest young lady turning into a cruel sensualist," screamed Miss Debrette, unable to restrain her cries, and yet urging her tormentor so as to hasten the access of pleasure.

Julia, blushing and crimson at what she is doing, yet seems to experience a thrilling sense of warmth and pleasure as each cut descends on the victim's flesh, she cuts away with all her might, making the olive tinted flesh look like a damask cheek of a full ripe peach, but scored in every direction with dark looking angry weals: "how obstinate; how insulting; I really will try to subdue your pride; now I see your blood slowly trickling from the weals.... Ah! I can't express myself.... but every strike gives me quite a strange pleasure.... I.... I.... I'll kill you if you don't apologise!" exclaimed Julia, as rage and a confused sense of shame seemed to make her almost beside herself.

All the company were in ecstasies of voluptuous excitement, but the Colonel was sufficiently collected to continue his suggestions and threats in Julia's ear, so that although she really was willing enough to punish Miss Debrette in the cruellest manner, she felt that her tormentor was deriving a double satisfaction in mortifying her modesty at the same time.

"Cut away; make your birch cut her dark hairy pussy in front; slash round her hips!" he hissed in her ear. "Ask how she likes such loving touches! if it doesn't make her feel funny; speak up, Julia, or by all the powers of heaven you shall rue it, Miss!" he said in another ferocious kind of whisper.

Julia (trembling from both fear and excitement): "Ah! She shall feel.... She shall feel..., if her impudent obstinacy does not give way. There! There!! There!!!" slashing three most painful cuts exactly as ordered by the Colonel, drawing the blood from the tender belly of the victim who fairly writhed in agony for a moment or two and then seemed to be unconscious of further pain, although Julia fairly flayed her richly coloured buttocks till they were bruised and bleeding all over; the victim sighing and giving little cries of excitement rather than of pain, till her head droops and she falls into a lethargy of blissful oblivion, whilst the spectators can actually see the proofs of her enjoyment as the spendings and blood trickle down her thighs in a mingled stream.

Colonel (in a fit of excitement): "Seeing is believing, but tasting is better," as he passes his hand over the slimy lips of the victim's cunny, which can just be seen from where they stand behind her, the pouting lips of her vagina throbbing in a kind of spasmodic ecstasy. "Here, Julia, open your mouth and taste it, it is exactly the same as what you told us happened to yourself. Ha! Ha!! You keep your lips closed, then, there!" as he wipes his fingers on her mouth. "Now, young lady, it is not only the floggee but the flogger who also experiences this voluptuous pleasure of enjoying yourself?" as he gloats over the awful confusion which his disgusting action and question have brought upon poor Julia, who is sobbing at her degradation and quite unable to find words to express her horror.

"Now, do you, dear girl?" he exclaims, giving her a tremendous cut with his whip on the tight fitting drawers which cover her bottom. "I'll soon cut through your rage if you don't speak," repeating his blow again and again, till she shrieks fearfully and runs in and out between the ladies and gentlemen to avoid his blows, till he drives her into a corner and makes her dance what he facetiously calls a whip hornpipe, Julia, screaming: "Mercy! Mercy!! O! I will do anything; I will! I will!! Oh!! Oh!!!"

"Then," said the Colonel, "step into the middle of the place and open your drawers in front, mind, no hesitation; his lordship shall tell us if you have experienced sensual pleasure or not."

The black-bearded gentleman instantly kneels down by her side with every appearance of devotion and sympathy as soon as she has assumed the proper position, saying: "Permit me, dear Julia, you know all my tenderness, and no one has such a good right to investigate your charms; don't blush so, dearest, we shall soon be married; why should my attentions confuse you so?" as he steadily watches her agitated features, and in reality finds exquisite pleasure at the sight of her distress; his hands pull aside the envious front of her chemise, which hides her mossy mount, even after her nervous fingers have opened the slit of her drawers in front. "Ah! What beauties! Did ever any one see such a soft golden chevelure of curly hair covering the grotto of love; and then, dearest, I can see the coral lips of your pussy just peeping out, as if impatient of being quite kept out of sight, and... Ah! Ah!! How they glisten with the dew of love. What better proof could we have of your ability to feel and confer pleasure; 'tis the real nectar from your virgin fount," tickling her with his fingers and then excitedly sucking them as if it was the most delicious treat in the world.

This is an awful ordeal to Julia who seems to drink the very dregs of shameful degradation, as her brimming eyes encounter the delighted looks of all around her, and she feels they are gloating over her moral torture; all the whipping and painful punishments have not eradicated a particle of her innate modesty, which this outrage seems to make more sensitive than ever.

Colonel. — "Ha! This is exquisite, and I see you have all fully appreciated my lecture thus far. I think the first part of my theory has been exceedingly well illustrated by Miss Ponsonby, her flagellation of our lady friend did her great credit, and I feel sure after marriage she will prove an artiste very worthy of our society. Now we will rest for a few minutes, whilst some one gives a relation of their experiences, but first Julia must be secured to the ladder ready for me to renew the lecture in its last and serious part, viz, the flagellation in earnest; we have up to this point been comparatively playful, and amused ourselves more by studying the mental than the bodily phase of the subject. Tie her up to the ladder, with her back to the rings, secure her ankles so that her toes cannot touch the ground, and her arms well stretched and secured high above her head; let all the strain of her weight be on the wrists and ankles, only slightly relieved by her back being inclined against the ladder," then, seeing that his lordship and the captain had exactly carried out his ideas in the arrangement of the victim, he added: "That was a favourite position of the Grand Inquisitors in Spain, they used to fix up a young lovely victim in that painful manner, then sit before her for a long time, whilst one of their acolytes would read descriptions of fearful and shameful tortures and outrages to which previous young ladies had been subjected, the Chief Inquisitors stopping the reading every now and then to ask their terrified and horror stricken victim how she would like "so and so" or, perhaps, something a little more degrading would suit you better, &c."

"I will tell you a little more about their practices before this is over."

PART THE SECOND

After a little refreshment the Colonel observes "that he thinks Miss Debrette is sufficiently recovered to relate a little of her experiences, but he hopes that her smarting bottom will not distract her ideas too much."

The lady in the black domino when thus appealed to thanks him for his consideration, saying: "I will let you all into an excellent secret, by which anyone whose poor posteriors have been flayed as mine have, not only gets instant relief but can sit quite comfortably at once. I have a short light quilted down petticoat, the inner surface of which has been rubbed all over with a most cooling ointment, made of cold cream, mixed with tincture of arnica, and as soon as my flogging is over I slip it on next to my raw skin and dispense with my drawers till the next day; you cannot imagine how cool and comfortable it is, and how quickly I am ready for another delicious whipping; now, I will go on with a little incident which has recurred to my recollection, and may, perhaps, afford you some amusement."

"You don't want to know when it happened, but I

was once upon a visit to a young widow in the country, who had been an old schoolfellow; the second night of my stay in her house I was astonished, when, after supper, just as we were going to retire, she asked, in a manner which clearly implied my presence was neither expected or desired: "If I was willing to attend prayers?" "No, thanks, Bella, dear, and I should think you had enough of that sort of thing at school," I replied as I took my candle, thinking it was somewhat strange there were no prayers the previous night, and I soon found out as the days went on that she only had prayers every other night, which was a curious puzzle to me. At school we had never had any secrets, but now she was very reticent, and I determined secretly to examine into her half system of piety rather than question her upon the subject.

I never let things wait, when I once make up my mind, so next morning, whilst my young widow was gone to call upon a sick neighbour, I quietly investigated the room where she usually retired with her footman (a handsome fellow of two and twenty), and the three female servants all young and good looking. There was a fine large couch, besides an easy chair and other seats, on the table lay a fine family bible, and also a book of domestic devotion, but which to me looked singularly new and unused; this made me look carefully into the cupboard where I found three or four fine new birch rods quite ready for use. Enlightened at once by this discovery, but how to get a view of my friend's precious prayer-meeting; was she a female Cornelius Hadrien making her servants pray and submit to flagellation at her hands; I must see for myself; it was a comfortable kind of breakfast parlour in the lowest part of the house, whilst I slept two flights higher up, and was no doubt supposed to be quite safe in my room before their prayers commenced;

the room had a half glass-door, furnished with a silken curtain inside, stretched tightly from two small brass rods at top and bottom upon which it could easily be slipped a little at the side or one corner if desired. My first care was to purchase a pair of slippers with list soles so that I could walk the passages and go up or down stairs quite noiselessly, then, previous to the next evening for prayers, I managed during the day to draw slightly the curtain at the lower corner so as only to leave a small aperture not likely to be noticed.

Upon retiring to my bedroom after wishing my friend good night, I purposely made as much noise as possible in bolting myself in (I had been purposely talking of burglars to make them think I was timid), but in reality leaving the bolt back so as I could quietly open the door. Rapidly divesting myself of my boots and rustling silk skirts, I slipped on a warm dressing gown and my list slippers, then silently opening the door went down stairs a few steps and listened. I heard Bella ask Robert if he had seen all safe, and then say: "Come on all of you; Miss Debrette has bolted herself in, we need not wait so long this evening." I waited till they had all retired to the breakfast parlour, and then, hearing the key turned in the lock, at once quietly descended and took my place outside the glass door, where I could see all over the room.

It was a curious kind of prayer meeting; Robert was rapidly divesting himself of his coat, trousers, and vest, whilst my friend, Bella, and her three pretty domestics were also slipping off their things, so that they soon stood in nothing but chemise, drawers, &c., and I also noticed that the three pretty servants had their under clothing, hose and boots of the most elegant and exquisite quality, no doubt at my friend's expense; it was a rare sight for me, as I dote upon a girl in drawers, and am sure that ladies, although supposed to be used to the sight, quite appreciate all the ideas we have heard from the Colonel and the Captain this evening. Well, to go on with my story, the first act of devotion was my friend taking a good birch from her cupboard, as she asked, "whose turn it was to be first this evening."

"It's me, Mar'm," said Hannah, a sprightly looking brunette of about nineteen, as she turned down her eyes under the ardent gaze of Mr. Robert, and seemed to blush for shame.

"Hand her to the sofa, then, Sir, without any more delay. Jane shall horse Polly on her back and present a double bum to my birch, and the sight will do us all a little good."

They pushed the table from the centre of the room close up to the wall, and then Jane, leaning her body forward over the shining mahogany, presented a finely rounded bottom just over the edge of the table, and her feet, stretched wide apart, were tied by her fellow servant by the ankles to the legs of the table, then Polly opened the drawers behind, and turned them down so that at least half of the thighs were exposed.

Madame Bella (whisking her rod impatiently): "Make haste and seat yourself, and then we can at once jog on."

Meanwhile Robert was trying to incline the blushing Hannah backwards on the sofa, but she did not like the position, protesting that it prevented both of them seeing nicely how Madame was using her rod. "Let me lean forward over the head of the sofa, and be on my knees, so you can have me dog fashion, I love it so that way, it's more exciting and not so likely to do mischief," she added, giving his affair a loving squeeze. His shirt prevented me seeing the actual act of coition between them, and her drawers were only just opened sufficiently to admit his advance, still their excited motions and flushed faces were a most voluptuous treat to see, especially when she twisted her head round to kiss and suck his tongue at the ecstatic moment when he seemed to shoot his very life into her. I am getting ahead of the other actors in my relation, although the others were equally busy at the same time. Polly had mounted on Jane's back and had given her hands to the latter, who held them in front of her by the wrists, whilst the mistress had carefully opened the drawers, and exposed another fine rump by tucking the drawers out of sight under the girl's belly in front, whilst the chemise was pinned up to the shoulders. The double bum presented a pretty contrast in the way of complexion, Jane, the cook, was a pretty red-haired young woman of twenty-five, with the whitest possible skin, and her fine plump buttocks looked all the prettier for a few freckles, the light brown spots making it peculiarly attractive, and then again (it seems such a rude thing to mention but I must tell my story properly) she had a deliciously pink bottom hole, whilst underneath could just be seen the cherry lips of her cunny nestled in a thicket of light reddish hair. Polly's posteriors were beautifully white and firm, but not quite so large as the fine rump she bestrode, she was a nice looking girl of twenty-one, with pale face, but hair and eyes as dark as night, and there was the peculiar difference in the kind of whiteness of her skin, which is so perceptible in dark people however delicate their complexion may be, whilst her little wrinkled hole was shaded round by the darkest possible brown, and a luxuriant growth of black hair quite hid her crack from sight. As this lecture by the Colonel is to elucidate all kinds of voluptuous facts, I may remark that it's a curious circumstance in relation to the chevelure of ladies' affairs that the blackest are always furnished with the most luxuriant growth of long hair, whilst very fair girls generally have it so short, curly, and light, as to be of very little use for the purpose of screening their pouting charms. My friend applied her birch most vigorously so that both girls screamed: "Pity! Mercy! Oh! Oh! Ah-r-r-r-re! I can't bear it! Oh! Oh! Not so hard! Not so hard!!" Jane was held fast by Polly's wrists and her bottom wriggled in the most delightful manner under the smarting cuts which Bella administered with such artistic skill as to raise a beautiful dark red flush all over the two bottoms without breaking the skin. It would take too long to relate how Polly took Hannah on her back whilst Robert had Jane on the sofa; the latter was a most luscious love encounter as the red-haired beauty had her naturally voluptuous temperament so excited by her birching; how she hugged the footman to her bosom and entwined her lustful limbs over his buttocks; I am sure he deluged her with his sperm at least three times, and only let her go most reluctantly when Polly had to take her place and my friend again run the changes with the double bums; at last Robert had done with all three of the servants, and evidently knowing the regular routine of his mistress in her family devotions, seated himself for a minute or two on the sofa, till my friend had arranged the three girls into a treble bum one above the other; the cook with her fine rosy rump at the bottom, Jane astride of her buttocks, and Hannah on the top of her, a most delightful pyramid of blushing bums as they were all still smarting from the effects of the cuts.

The mistress takes up a pretty new light bunch of

twigs, Robert springs up from the sofa, throws off his shirt, displays his splendidly developed dart of love to my eyes in all its rampant glory, surrounded by a black fringe of hair; his silk stockings and fine elegant boots seem to set off his figure to great advantage, as, with a most graceful step, he advances to the rear of his mistress, and assists her to remove chemise and drawers.

Bella was a beautiful fair woman, only twenty-three, of the Venus height, pretty figure well rounded and developed without any superfluous fat; her blue eyes sparkled with amorous excitement as she turned and gave her man servant a most loving kiss, and then saying: "Mind, you hold me tight, Robert," turned her back to him; he seemed to lift her in his strong arms and seat her across his stiff affair, whilst she putting one hand behind her directed the excited member to the slit, her feet were off the ground, but he seemed to hold her easily in his iron grasp, as she delightedly wriggled upon his peg, and thrashed away with her birch on the treble bum making them keep up quite a lively chorus of cries under the smarting whisks; this was a most lascivious and exciting scene, and when I afterwards obtained her confidence by confessing to her what I had seen, she told me that her idea was to obtain the greatest possible pleasure without risk of pregnancy, which she did not think was very probable after the man had to satisfy her three servants; and her idea, besides giving her all the preliminary excitement of birching the double bums and seeing the delicious encounters with her girls, made his affair as stiff and strong from continued excitement, that there was very little limit to her indulgence as she might wriggle and plunge and spend upon it without pumping much more from his exhausted reservoir, in fact it went on till she felt fatigued with the combined exertions of coition and flagellation.

That is the end, and I shall not satisfy your curiosity any further as to whether I joined in the family prayers or not, whilst I remained in the home, but I always recollect it as the most luscious thing I ever saw or heard in my life."

They are all delighted with this anecdote, and thank the lady most enthusiastically; the Colonel observing that it has been a beautified illustration of the fantastic style which he had already enlarged upon.

Old blue-beard says: "I have known some curious people in my time, especially in reference to drawers, one was a gentleman, a widower (pray, do not imagine I am speaking of myself as you all know what an innocent reputation I have); well, he had an only daughter of fourteen, a good looking pretty girl, who was so cowed by his strict manner, that she would obey without a word anything he might fancy to order, and his favourite amusement was after dinner to sit over his dessert quietly smoking his cigar, whilst his daughter stood before him for half and hour or more, with her skirts well up so as to expose her drawers nearly up to her waist, he would lean back in his chair without a word, all the time enjoying the sight of her pretty arms as they were gradually dropping, then a sudden angry twitch of his eyebrows would frighten the poor girl into clutching up her petticoats again as she was so dreadfully afraid of the old gentleman, who gloated over the sight of her flushed face, brimming eyes, and puckering lips as she strove to restrain the sobs which she was afraid to give utterance to."

"Another one of my acquaintances was ready to go out of his mind if he could not find out whether a girl had drawers on or not, and what they were like; he would waylay young ladies going to school, and coming behind them turn their skirts over their heads and give two or three slaps on their bottom before they could recover or see their assailant; he was always differently dressed, and would be some distance off with his back to them when they looked round; he had a favourite plan of using a small walking stick with a curved handle so that he could put it right under the crack of their bottoms and hook out the tail of their chemise to see the complexion of their delicate flesh, and you can imagine that sometimes the hook would go into their pussies and almost kill the poor girls with the pain, shame and fright, in fact two or three were found lying insensible in the road or path, but were generally to ashamed to say much about how they had been treated; others fled in frantic terror, screaming for assistance. He carried on his game for months, till he thought it prudent to transfer the theatre of his operations to a distant locality."

The Captain. — "I think in a club like ours every one who has had any practical experiences ought to relate them for the general benefit, so I will tell you of the amusement I sometimes derive from associating with the lower classes down in the workman's neighbourhood, feigning to be one myself and properly disguised, I used to make friends with any particularly brutal sort of fellow by standing lots of beer, any one who will do that is one of the proper, jolly sort with such men. I well remember one fellow, a sadler by trade, whom I met one day in a low street just over London Bridge, he looked more like a brewer's man, but was going along the street with a fine bunch of twigs, tied up into a regular looking rod, as if he had just made it from a birch broom; it was carried under his arm as an officer would his sword; he had a pipe in his mouth, but what struck my fancy at once was a peculiar delighted look about his eyes, and he seemed almost ready to laugh, as he walked along evidently delighted at something he was picturing to himself. "I'd stand a pot to know what your game is with that tickler, old boy," I said. — "Nothing like me for the young uns, and old ooman allus gets the benefit of it arter, it's a rare go for whacking as well as making kids, I can tell-ee, my boy; stand another pot or two at my house and see the fun I gets out o'my gal." I soon made the bargain, and when we got into his dirty parlour sent out the wife for a pint of gin and half a gallon of beer. "Missis," said the brutal fellow, "where's our brat? My chum here wants to see the fun." The woman, who was tolerably good looking but with a very sensual cast of countenance, evidently had as much pleasure as her brutal husband in the whipping of the girl, and soon brought in a trembling little thing of about twelve years of age, who would have looked rather pretty if well dressed and cared for. The half drunken father seized her and throwing her across his knee used the birch with terrible effect; her shrieks and cries filled the whole place, and he only lets her down when his own arm ached from his exertions and the poor child ran out of the room with the raw weals on her buttocks streaming with blood till it trickled into her shoes. Another day the besotted brute, encouraged by my laughter, stripped the little Milly as he called her stark naked, laid her on the table face downwards, fastening her in such a manner that she could not move; then he amused himself by making her shriek in agony as he from time to time applied the bowl of his almost red hot pipe to her thin little bottom; then he knocked out the burning tobacco ashes, and left it smoking on her scorched skin, and finished this exquisitely refined exhibition of cruelty by taking a red hot coal from the fire and placing it on the right cheek of the victim's bottom, seating himself in his chair to enjoy the heart rending shrieks of the little thing, pointing out to me with a brutal chuckle every spasmodic movement of the little burning bum, saying the smell of cooked meat made him think the Missis had got something good for his supper; it really was a most voluptuous treat to watch all the "resserrements" of the victim as the French call it."

Colonel. — "That's more approaching the earnest style which is made up of downright hard whipping and serious torture: now look at our victim how she is amused by these tales; Julia, you look more interesting than ever, and I must now proceed to illustrate the second part of my lecture; I want these ladies and gentlemen to understand the beautiful effect of soft touches which I am going to begin with, but first I must pull down your drawers, a little action must be preferable to your painfully strained position."

He has taken up a fine bunch of fresh stinging nettles fixed in an elegant bouquet paper for a handle, he loosens her drawers, and pulls them down to her heels, so that, as her feet are rather wide apart, she looks as if she had linen shackles on; then taking a chair he sits down close in front of the victim.

Julia, who has heard all the previous tales, is in a dreadful state of apprehension, and more crimson than ever, the marks on her thighs have turned into a dull dark colour, and the tears are streaming down her distressed looking face, as her eyes are turned down to avoid the delighted looks of the company, who are in a state of expectant excitement.

Colonel (resuming): "We are now changing from the mental to the physical aspect of the lecture; in my previous remarks I have dwelt mostly upon the feeling of shame and degradation which such a modestly brought up young lady would feel at every exposure or humiliating order: now I come to the real bodily suffering to be caused by applications of whips, and any contrivance which will create intense pain; and if to that we can also add the mental element which we have been previously working upon, and which is never really exhausted in a such a sensitively modest young lady as Miss Ponsonby here; why, it will materially add to our voluptuous excitements as the lecture progresses, and my practical illustrations will bring out all the erotic propensities of these here present."

He begins to apply the nettles first round her hips and buttocks, which the victim bears without wincing.

Colonel. — "I'm only tickling her for a moment or two: you don't mind it yet, Miss Julia, it's not quite so bad as you expected: suppose I try a tenderer part: Eh! How do you like nettles applied to your ticklish little clitoris, Miss Ponsonby?"

Here he roughly thrusts the bunch right under her cunny and rubs them well in her slit, the pain is terrible, and horrified victim shrieks out: "Not there.... Oh! Oh!!... Ah-r-r-r-re!" with a long frantic yell of pain, and then again: "Stop! Stop!! For pity's sake. Sir! Oh! Not there again! Not there!! Ah-r-r-r-r-re!"

Colonel (with an excited laugh): "Ha! Ha! How you seem to enjoy it; do you mean there, Julia?" as he switches them right under her three times and draws the nettles painfully along her tender crack, and then goes on: Swish... Swish... Swish with the bunch, enjoying all her agonising contortions, and piercing cries.

Julia. — "Oh! Oh!! Oh!!! What shall I do? What shall I do? Oh! No! No!! No!!! Not again! Oh! Pity! Have mercy!" as she almost faints under this excruciating application of the nettles.

The Colonel throws away the nettles, and two of the Gentlemen release Julia from her painful position. His Lordship and old Blue-beard vying with each other in their assumed sympathy for the poor girl, chafing her ankles with their hands, and drawing on her pantaloons with great care and tenderness; it is an exquisite treat to them as they put the finishing touches to make her comfortable by tucking in her chemise all round her bottom, the Marquis taking great care to arrange the tail of her under-garment well over the smarting clitoris and the red looking lips of her virgin vagina.

They give her a glass of champagne, with about a teaspoonful of invigorating cordial, and then at a sign from the master of the ceremonies, she is again fixed up to the ladder with her back to the company, and the drawers are opened, pinned back on each side exposing her pretty bottom to the lecturer and audience, who can see the dark marks of the previous strokes of the whip; the Colonel now has a whip made of about two dozen long thin strips of moderately hard leather, fixed in an ornamental handle, and resuming his lecture, goes on to say:—

"For sensual cruelty and real degradation of their victims, nothing comes up to the old Inquisition in

Spain, that arch fiend Torquemada knew how to draw the greatest possible gratification for himself and colleagues from the sight of his suffering victims.

Their torture was inflicted in the most sensual manner; they would have a lovely trembling girl stripped stark naked, and her bottom carefully flayed, then whipped with nettles, then burnt with hot iron plates, and then the acolytes had to turn her round for them to gloat over her speechless agony; at first they would let the poor thing scream and enjoy the music of her cries, then, as the torture progressed, she was gagged to increase the horribly intense agony which they could see in her writhing face, and knowing the fact that agony which can not be expressed by cries, is doubled in its intensity by the victim's inability to let it off by her shrieks.

They amused themselves by every kind of insulting and obscene observations as to the victim's lewdness or chastity, had them whipped with scourges made from wire, every cut from which brought away pieces of flesh, and usually finished off a victim by pinching her all over with red hot pincers, beginning at the fingers and toes till the most vital parts were reached, every now and then stopping to prolong the torture, and enjoy the last spasmodic contortions of the victim; I could enlarge upon their cruelty, but it is too shocking, but there is one practice of theirs so awfully humiliating to a modest nature that I should like to mention it if you would not be too shocked."

Both ladies and gentlemen promise not to be offended, assuring him that every thing which relates to the creation of sensual feelings is perfectly in order between members of the society; Miss Debrette exclaiming: "We shall listen with breathless interest."

Colonel. — "Well, in one place they have trained dogs for the torture of their female victims. Ha! You don't seem to understand me, (he laughs); well, you must pardon my being excessively plain, they used to strip a girl and fasten her down to the floor by her hands and knees, so that she was what we call on all fours, the same as an animal, then she was cruelly scourged all over till her buttocks and loins were literally raw. Presumably an acolyte would bring in a large mastiff, the well trained dog at once going up to the horrified victim, licks the shrieking girl's naked body all over, delighting especially to thrust his long tongue under her bottom and into her crack in the most lasciviously exciting manner, the Inquisitors all the while taunting their victim about her brutish sensuality, and would read out to her well known texts from Leviticus about the shameful crime of women, who should kneel down before a beast. You can imagine the fearful agony and shame of the trembling victim, her piercing cries for death as a mercy, rather than have to submit to such dreadful infamy. After gloating over this scene as long as possible the chief inquisitor would give a signal which the well trained brute instantly obeyed by mounting its bleeding agonized victim, and.... I suppose I must speak it out, rape her, with all the impetuosity of his animal nature."

The ladies cover their faces and give a little scream of horror, they really can't believe such things could ever have been.

Colonel. — "All quite true I assure you, and done to uphold the glory and purity of the Roman Catholic Church, some of the monkish inquisitors would enjoy studying all the phases of suffering on the victim's face, whilst others delighted in watching the actual act of coition between the female and the dog, as the most exciting to their sensual natures. Try, if possible to realise to yourselves the crushed and degraded feelings of the poor girl as she was permitted to retire to her dungeon, and also that she knew this disgusting inhuman outrage would be repeated upon her chastity day by day till they finished her off; four or five times of this horror invariably killed a delicate modest minded girl. They had little dogs as well as some of the largest ones; for some of the victims were tender little girls of ten or twelve, and, as if this was not sufficiently atrocious, if a mother was in their hands she was stripped, flogged, and bound to a stake to witness the degradation of her child. Some of them took especial delight in the torture of little girls by letting them run loose in their large hall, having previously well scourged and flayed their bottoms, a large dog would be set to chase the terrified little victim; these dogs were so well trained that they would bite the bottoms of the victim without inflicting any fatal injury, and, if called upon, would fetch the little things by the buttocks in all their writhing agony and lay them at the feet of their masters like well-trained retrievers with game. The sight of the thin white haggard features of the little girls as they were dying by inches day by day amused these extraordinary sensualists."

Colonel (after a slight pause): "Luckily for you, Julia, we have no trained dogs; what a delicious sight it would be to see you run screaming round this place, with a fine mastiff biting your pretty bottom or touching up your lewd clitoris with his long tongue; but I must not let it sink too much into your mind, these little leather straps will make you forget every thing for a moment. Do they sting as well as the nettles, Miss Ponsonby?" he asks as the first whisk of the whip brings the leather tips in smarting contact with her bottom, leaving a lot of red spots to mark the effect: "There! There!! There!!!;" he repeats as each cut is increased in force, till the victim writhes and screams in exquisite pain.

Julia. — "Ah! Ah!! Oh! Oh!! Oh!!! Ah-r-r-r-re! Will you never have pity? Ah-r-r-r-re! Each thing is worse than the last! I shall die; I can't bear it!" as she twists about under the scratching cuts.

Colonel. — "You must bear it!" Swish... swish... swish. "Ha! a spot of blood!" Swish... swish... swish... "It will soon trickle down the white flesh of your thighs, and, perhaps, to your feet. I think after all I should like to see you caper; will you oblige by setting one leg at liberty and pulling the drawers down to her heels" (addressing the Captain).

This is done and the chemise pinned up, then again swish... swish... as the leather tips wind round her bottom and buttocks.

Colonel. — "Ha! Ha!! They do cut a little, eh, Julia? The virgin blood is trickling finely now... I'll have the little riding whip again, please."

Julia. — "Oh: Mercy! Mercy!! Spare me! Will nobody have pity? I feel as if burnt with hot irons," here she breaks down, and is almost choked with hysterical sobs.

Colonel. — "What did you think about those dogs, Julia? Speak out; we want to know your thoughts; there's something to make you collect your ideas, Miss," giving the poor girl a fearful cut up under her bottom, so as to draw the blood from the tender lips of her cunny. "How do you like it there yourself; I noticed you took great pleasure in giving these undercuts when you handled the birch; now, answer, answer, answer!" with a stroke at each word cutting terrible weals on the inside of her tender thighs.

The excruciating pain, together with the dreadful sense of degrading humiliation, had such an effect on the victim that, although she plunged and writhed and gave fearful screams, she was perfectly unable to even gasp out a reply to his questions.

Here the Colonel was afraid she might faint too soon, so the whip was stayed whilst a few drops of the cordial were poured down Julia's parched throat; then going on again, he says: "That's right, she must not faint yet; perhaps, Julia, you can find your tongue now, or I'll cut the flesh off your bones with this whip," as he goes whack.... whack.... whack, but not quite so hard as before.

Julia (frightened with distress): "Was ever misery like this? Such torments of body mixed with unspeakable mental horror; these outrages on my sense of modesty are worse than all the tortures you can think of or inflict; you ask my thoughts about such awful things, I can but describe them by saying how degraded I felt at being compelled to listen to every word of your fearful tale; your words are as distressing as your cruel cuts, each one of which makes me wish for death, to release me from such abominable humiliations.... Oh! Oh!! Are all your hearts steeled against pity? Do women revel in such cruel outrages on modesty and decency as well as men? Oh! May the earth rather swallow me up and hide my awful shame!"

Her eyes are streaming with tears, and the muscles of her bottom still quiver from the effects of the whip and scourge, whilst her face, which, as she said this, was mostly looking towards the ladies, had a most sorrowful expression, relieved each instant by a burning blush, deeper and deeper still as she so pathetically depicted her shame and sense of degradation; the effort to speak was finally too much for her; a thick mist seemed to obscure her vision, so that all around seemed laughing gibbering demons glorying in her sufferings; she could say no more; her head turned once more to the ladder as she gave vent to a succession of broken hearted sobs.

Colonel. — "Poor thing, this lecture is rather too strong for her innocent nerves; what was that one of you, ladies, suggested to me a few minutes ago?"

Lady Curzon (in the red domino): "Oh! Do let the poor girl down for a little! It's deliciously exciting, dear Julia, it makes me love you with an indescribable yearning, and I long to see more of it, and want to see you walk round just as you are, with your drawers dragging about your heels; Colonel, dear, just as you did before: March! March!! Early in the morning, you will remember."

Colonel. — "Just so; it will refresh her a little; Julia, you hear what her ladyship wishes" (they untie her hands and feet); "now gather the chemise under your arms and walk round, so as we can see the effects of your punishment so far. Step out! Step out!!" touching her bottom with smart little applications of his whip. "What graceful action! Don't stumble!" as the draggling drawers almost throw the poor girl down as she capers at each stinging cut: "Hold up! Don't jump so! I'm sure you've no cause to be so restive!" as he laughingly switches in front of her delicate mount, till the blood can be seen hanging in little drops to the light curly chevelure of her pussy: "Halt!" shouts the Colonel in a loud voice. "You've seen boys playing at leap frog: stand still and make a back, these gentlemen would like to fly over you."

The poor girl is so cowed she instantly obeys, and the first three gentlemen bound over her back in succession with the lightest possible touch, but old Crim-Con purposely bungles so as to bring both himself and the victim to the ground.

Colonel (in assumed rage) whips the without mercy as she lies on the floor, exclaiming: "Take that! and that!! and that!!! You've hurt the gentleman by your giving way under him." He cuts her everywhere over her head, face, neck, bosom, legs, and feet, delighted to see her writhe about in agony, whilst her screams of pain echoed through the conservatory with thrilling and piercing effect; at last, after enjoying her exquisite agony for a few moments, he orders her to make another back for himself, and as she once more assumes the bent position, steps back a pace or two, as if for a run, but instead of going over the victim passes behind giving a terrific running cut which completely doubles poor Julia up with pain, eliciting a regular screech of anguish, and also a little cry of excitement from the ladies who had been looking on with breathless interest.

This last cut raised an awful looking weal right across the victim's buttocks, and along its line the bruised skin oozed with little drops of blood.

"I think," said the Colonel, wiping the perspiration from his forehead, "that was a practical illustration of flogging in earnest; we all require a drop of champagne and I hope his lordship won't forget Miss Julia, those little attentions will cement the very natural affection she must begin to feel for him. Ha! Ha!! Ha!!! What a joke to see one's bride well whipped, and done her wedding night, but his lordship is one of the lucky ones, as I warrant she is learning to love, honour, and obey, and will say it with unfeigning lips when the clergyman begins his office. Well, we all wish his lordship every joy with such a charming partner; Miss Julia will be in the best possible condition and temperament to reciprocate his love between the sheets. This wedding puts me in mind of another curious tale. I once heard of an old millionaire about sixty who had a fancy to amuse himself with a poor, but beautiful girl of nineteen; after a hasty marriage they travelled through Italy and went to a secluded villa belonging to him, deep in the gorge of the Appenines, his only attendant being a young footman of eighteen, named Charles.

He had given secret orders, and everything had been arranged to further his plans for amusement. The young wife was very much struck by the absence of servants, and still more surprised at finding a real Berkeley Horse in their bedroom, which gave rise to the following exciting incident.

Wife, examining the horse with considerable curiosity: "My dear, what on earth is that thing for: is not it a pair of steps?"

Husband, with a chuckle of delight: "Yes, Rosa, it's a pair of steps, on purpose for you to walk up and let me see your legs and point out your beauties to my valet Charles."

Wife, incredulously, and thinking her husband is only

joking, yet slightly flushing with indignation at the idea of being exposed before the man-servant: "That you never will, Sir; I'd have the ugly thing knocked to pieces and burnt first," getting still more indignant as she sees that there is something in the wind, from his curious twinkling eyes, and quiet subdued chuckle.

Husband. — "Is that the way you keep your promise to love, honour, and obey, Madame? Suppose I order you to undress this instant to your chemise and drawers like a naughty school girl, and stretch yourself out on that thing ready for the rod; how would you like it, eh?"

Wife, with rising indignation and not yet being aware of his real character: "You might order for a long time before I should think proper to obey; that is anything but applicable to the kind of obedience women are supposed to owe their loving spouses."

Husband. — "I'm the best judge of that, and you will obey my slightest whim, unless you would rather I had to shoot you on the spot, a man can do anything with his wife in a place like this. Strip.... Strip.... Strip, to your drawers this instant or I will fire," presenting a loaded pistol at her bosom.

Wife, with a scream of terror: "Ah-r-r-r-r-re! Oh! Oh!! For Heaven's sake, don't point that deadly thing at me;" as she draws back in horror.

Husband, with a fierce look: "Do as I tell you or I will put a bullet through your heart," following up the terrified girl as she retreats to the wall of the apartment.

Wife, awfully scared: "I will! I will! Oh! Spare my life! What must I do, Sir?" going on her knees.

Husband, with a furious kick on her bottom: "Get up! Get up!! Off with your dress and petticoats, and do exactly as I order. I'll teach you to obey me. It's best to take all pride and obstinacy out of a wife at first."

The poor thing springs up hardly knowing what she is about, pulling off her things in a dreadful hurry, for fear he may call Charles to act as lady's maid, as he threatens.

Husband. — "Now, Madame, step on the footboard of what you call my pair of steps; but it's a horse, do you understand? A horse for you to ride, whilst a good rod will regulate the motions of your bottom, and acquaint your delicate posteriors with the virtue of birch discipline."

The young wife, blushing for shame, and tears coursing over her crimsoned face, is afraid to hesitate, and steps up as she feelingly appeals: "You really cannot mean it! Oh! Pray, Sir, don't humiliate me so! You will find me always loving and obedient!" But there is no pity in his looks, she is ordered to tie one wrist herself to a ring well above her head, and then the old man, laying his pistol on a table, secures the other wrist and also one ankle tightly to a ring at the foot, the wife all the while piteously begging him not to carry his joke to far. — "Pray, pray, be merciful! Oh, you can't be a going to hurt me!" she sobs hysterically.

Husband, ironically: "Hurt you! Only make a few fine weals on your bottom, and let out a little of obstinate blood; at least Charles will do it (ringing the bell) it's too fatiguing for me, and I shall enjoy looking on best; what do you think I married you for? For your smirking face, eh? No, no, you never made a greater mistake, it was to invigorate my used up energies by the sight of your suffering. Ha! Ha!! Ha!!! You little thought of that when you sold yourself to a rich old man."

His wife is quite overwhelmed with shame and confusion as the valet now entered the room with a couple of fine birches, she is crimson to the roots of her hair, and shuts her eyes to avoid seeing the young man's astonished delighted looks.

Husband. — "Will you please ask Charles to open your drawers, so as your bottom is properly bared to the rod; say, "Undo my drawers, Charles, please.""

Wife is too agitated to do anything but shriek out: "Help! Help!! Oh! For shame! Let me down! I won't, I won't be whipped!"

Husband, delighted at her fright and shame: "But you must be whipped, my dear, I begin quite to dote upon you; I feel for all your shame and humiliation; it makes my usually chill blood begin to thrill through my veins with unusual warmth, which nothing but such a sight could have done; I would not spare you for all the world, it's too delicious."

Tears, shrieks for help as well as entreaties are all unavailing, he threatens to shoot her, if she does not ask the valet to "undo her drawers." The old fellow gets so impatient that he strikes her several times with a cane over her bare shoulders leaving dark red bruises, and heedless of her cries for mercy keeps on till at last she falters out: "Oh! Oh!! Charles please to open my drawers!" the husband laughing at the success of his caning remarks: "Now mind, Charles, put them well back and put the tail of her chemise out of the way so that it does not interfere with the effects of your birch."

Thus admonished the valet, delighted with his

task, paid particular attention to the careful exposition of his mistress' beautiful bottom, the poor young lady all the while sobbing for shame, or expressing her sense of the indignity in subdued expressions, such as: "How dare you touch me, Charles? O! Oh!! Let me alone for shame! Let your master do it himself! How degrading! I can never look up again!" Her confusion increasing till at last she seems going to faint.

Husband. — "What a pretty bum! Would you believe me, Charles, that's the first time I have been allowed to look at it, but see, she's likely to faint, all her blood has flown to her face, make haste and draw it back to that pretty plump bottom," delighted at the increasing distress of his victim.

Wife, in terror. "Ah! No! No!! Oh! No! I can't bear it! Oh! Let me down; you surely cannot carry such a horrid joke any further," then, as she feels the first light switch: "Charles, Charles, pray, don't hit me very hard, my skin is so tender," tears of shame and mortification coursing down her burning cheeks.

Husband. — "Go on! Go on!! Never mind a little whimpering and screaming: Ha! Ha!! That's better! Put a little more force into your blows!" getting quite excited as the peach-like bloom of the first strokes gradually deepens into a damask shade, set off with a lot of angry looking weals.

The valet is almost as excited as his master, the more the lady screams and cries for mercy the more he cuts on the excoriated bum, till at last the ruby drops ooze from the lacerated weals and trickle over the flesh; here the old gentleman hastily interposes, observing: "I shall lose half the pleasure if I can't see it run over the white flesh of her thighs; now, cut away again my boy," rubbing his withered hands in delight, as the wife writhes about and kicks frantically with the disengaged leg, as each smarting stroke adds to her agony and shame.

Husband, with a delighted chuckle: "Now, will you obey better in future? Will you admit I am the best judge of what is proper? Make the obstinate jade speak out, Charles," gesturing in his excitement for the valet to cut her up between the thighs and tenderest parts.

Their victim promises and shrieks by turns, but nothing stops the rod, till she has fainted under her exquisite suffering, and they have at last to lay her in bed in a state of insensibility.

The sequel to this tale is that the old gentleman died very mysteriously within three or four days after this humiliation of his young wife. The lady succeeded to a good share of his large fortune, and very soon after married the valet Charles; this incident would never have come to light had not one of his executors afterwards found a written account of the delicious scene in which the old man's own writing finished off with a note at the end to the effect, that she would not last long, the excitement was too delicious to spare his victim, and that he should soon have to look out for another wife.

Julia, although so painfully cut about, had not been seriously hurt, and all her thoughts were soon engrossed by this tale, whilst shame and fear of what was going to happen to herself, kept her in a continual state of agitation, as she crouched at the foot of the horse making her chemise cover as much as possible of her nakedness.

Colonel (turning to their victim): "I think Miss

Ponsonby would feel more comfortable in a fresh pair of drawers, my lord will you kindly assist her to step into these? They may be rather tight fitting but your gallantry will suggest how to arrange that most comfortably for your fiancée," handing the black-bearded gentleman a rather small looking pair of fine lawn pantaloons trimmed with most delicate lace.

Mr. Black-Beard, taking them, goes on one knee before Julia saying: "Allow me, Miss Ponsonby, to assist you in putting these on; will you please stand up and step into them; never mind, dear Julia, what you may expose to me, I will cover you as much as possible from other prying eyes."

Julia, all her delicate sensitiveness rushing to her face in repeated blushes, as she sobs for shame, makes haste to obey, saying in a low broken voice: "Oh! Sir, pray, turn your head, I can't bear you to look at my limbs so," looking down in the greatest confusion, as if it was the first exposure she had had to experience.

Colonel, with assumed anger: "Speak up, Miss; no whispering, everything must be spoken out for the benefit of the company," whisking about a leather scourge tipped with fine steel points as fine as pins, which glitter in the brilliant light of the place.

The victim puts one leg into the drawers which are so tight as with difficulty to admit her plump thigh after considerable persuasion and smoothing from his lordship's hands, then the same has to be gone through with the other leg, and they fit so tightly across her pretty rump, that although furnished with buttons behind, the delicate flesh can be seen peeping through the interstices, and the chemise has to be pinned up in a roll round her waist, it being impossible otherwise to dispose of it, the drawers being so tight that they look as if the least motion would split the fine material.

Colonel. — "Turn her round, I want to see if the hair of her pussy is all properly covered." Julia blushes deeper that ever, this tight pair of drawers seem to her so ludicrously humiliating and she knows they do not cover her in the most delicate parts; the Colonel continues: "Ha! Just as I expected; why, Julia your slit and the tip of your lewd clitoris are quite exposed, the sooner I cut such a pair of drawers off the better."

The gentlemen surround the poor girl, and understanding the Colonel's programma, turn her upside down and fasten her to the horse head downwards by one ankle and at the bottom by one wrist, patting and kissing her bottom as they do so, and taking all kinds of liberties with the horrified girl, who shrieks in great terror as she is adjusted in this position.

Colonel. — "Now I can again resume the practical illustration of the earnest style of whipping, this scourge which you see made of small strips of leather tipped with fine steel points, is an instrument which inflicts terrible agony, but if skilfully handled does not do serious harm, it will crimson her buttocks all over with her virgin blood, and I shall cut those flimsy drawers to rags but that will be all, unless, perhaps, Miss Ponsonby should treat us to a genuine fainting fit, but don't let alarm you, she will soon revive, and come up again quite reinvigorated by our careful applications of restoratives and stimulant. Look at that touch; see the little specks of blood instantly stain through the thin texture of the lawn, but they are only slight pin pricks, observe the effect of every lash, it may look terrible, but it's more in imagination than in reality."

His first light application of the steel tipped scourge is more startling than painful in its effects, poor Julia indeed winces every time it strikes, as it is impossible to prevent showing that she does feel it.

Colonel. — "Observe well all her writhings and contortions, those tight drawers show us every muscle as well as if she was quite naked, but they also answer the purpose of increasing her shame and mental degradation, as at every cut the victim dreads they may split or still further expose her delicate charms, is it not so, Julia? Tell us if you now feel the dregs of humiliation?" giving as a wind up to his question a terribly hard cut round her buttocks, making his tips of steel puncture all over her tender mount, which is instantly suffused with little drops of blood all over its surface, and hanging like dew from the short curly hair.

Julia shrieks in agony, but not in time to avert two or three more cuts like the last, one of which makes her clitoris spurt with blood which has collected in the cellular tissues of that excitable part, she shrieks out again and again in excruciating agony: "Oh! Oh!! Oh!!! Kill me in mercy; let me die now! Ah-r-r-re!"

Colonel. — "Will you answer, please, Miss Ponsonby, we want to know (especially the ladies) what you think of your shameful position, didn't that last cut warm your feeling a little? Eh! speak out!" as he cuts again and again on her tight looking bum, making the blood-saturated material of the drawers rend and crack under the effects of his strokes and the twisting of the victim.

Victim. — "Ah-r-r-r-re! Mercy! Mercy!! How can I tell my awful feelings?" then, as his cuts seem really killing her, she screams: "Oh! Oh!! It's far worse than my tongue can tell! I'm only fit to die now; you can't inflict a greater humiliation than this; I feel the very ache of despair and shame! Oh! How I smart and burn, I can't describe!" Then she breaks down into low sobs, whilst all the company are rapt in silent yet excited awe, as the dull sounds of the scourge mingle with this hysterical weeping.

The drawers are in tatters and the ensanguined surface of her buttocks look as if really flayed, the blood dripping and clotting all over her rent pantaloons and delicate legs even down to her boots.

Colonel. — "This has been an eminently practical bit of flagellation, now, suppose we let her down and refresh the poor girl with a little drop more of my wonderful cordial; make her kneel down, and every lady should provide herself with a good rod."

The gentlemen soon carry out this arrangement, with the victim kneeling in the centre of the place, whilst the four ladies pin up their skirts so as to show their beautiful legs and feet, and wait impatiently for the Colonel to proceed as they playfully whisk the twigs about.

Colonel. — "Miss Ponsonby, you seemed just now to think it impossible to be yet more humiliated, and little suspected this new degradation for your sensitive modesty: look up, I've got the ladies riding whip again; pull your chemise over your head. Never mind how the damaged drawers may happen to hang round your sore rump, all your attention is required in front, we, five gentlemen, are so excited and stiffened by the sight of your lewd contortions and delicious exposures, that we must be relieved; each one of us is going to present his rampant affair to your lips for a loving kiss, you must take them in your hand, rubbing and kissing them in turn as quickly as possible or this whip shall slash you to ribbons. Now then, Sir, present arms, and fire into her face as you are ready, if altogether it will increase our fun and her shame; ladies, ladies, do your duty to us behind!"

All the breeches were dropped in an instant, each male member holding up his shirt and coat tails behind, whilst the ladies thrashed away with their birches on the tough bottoms presented to their view; it would be impossible to describe properly this salacious scene. Julia's horror stricken, shamefaced looks, as the Colonel slashes over her shoulders till she begins to carry out his directions; he makes her take the head of each pego fairly in her mouth, and also use her light fingers as dexterously as possible; the poor girl is distracted and does not seem to know what she is doing, but mechanically obeys his fierce orders, "to use her tongue more, and not forget to play with her fingers."

The ladies are as excited as the gentlemen, now and then giving sly and painful cuts on the stiffened organs of their friends, which, with the weals in the rear, have such an exciting effect that the Colonel feels himself coming and calls out to the others to join in the fusillade as he shoots his sperm into the poor girl's gasping mouth, the others join in and Julia's blushing countenance is deluged with the life giving juice of love, even the old Marquis keeps company, his enervated nature is so reinvigorated by all he has experienced during the lecture: the slimy streams run all over the victim's neck and bosom, and this last indignity is so awfully degrading, that she sobs and gasps for breath for a moment or two and finally drops to the floor in a second death-like swoon.

The victim was left on the floor for a few minutes whilst the members of the society mingled in an indiscriminate orgy of voluptuous excesses, the last scene having quite demoralised both ladies and gentlemen, who were now obliged to give rein to their erotic passions in order to reduce themselves to a cooler state by letting off the steam of their excitement.

Colonel (who is the first to recover his equanimity): "Miss Julia will be all the better for her rest; now, gentlemen, apply some of those pungent salts to her nostrils, and rub a little on the palms of her hands, a friend of mine brought it from Constantinople, where they always keep it ready to restore any poor thing they may have to whip for the Sultan's pleasure or excitement, and I can vouch for its being a most marvellous reviver. Whilst she is coming round I will tell you how I first experimented with it, about a year ago I had a snug little hunting box in the country, and my housekeeper (who is a very demure staid sort of person left in charge by the gentleman I hired the place from) had a pretty dark-eyed daughter about twelve years of age; this little girl at once took my fancy as a most delicious little victim to operate upon with a birch: but how to manage it? They were almost independent of me, although I had three other nice female servants who were quite in my confidence."

Here the ladies tittered and seemed quite horrified at the Colonel, exclaiming: "Oh! Oh!! Did you ever know such an English Turk! Oh! For shame don't mention it, Sir!" &c.

Colonel, not all abashed: "I'm sure, ladies, some of you only want to look a little nearer home to find I'm not worse than many others, both ladies or gentlemen, for let me assure you there are female Turks who can easily accommodate themselves to three or four husbands or lovers at once: besides I have to thank my former salaciousness for bringing me into that rather enervated state which made me turn to these delightful experiments and practical illustrations for the purpose of occasionally warming my blood up to the requisite heat for voluptuous emotions."

Lady Manvers. — "Indeed, Colonel, dear, we did not mean anything serious, as we find you a most delightful instructor, and would be sorry to have you different; excuse our joking remarks, they were intended rather as a compliment to your manly abilities than otherwise; was it not so, ladies?"

All the Ladies. — "Yes! Yes! What should we do but for a few such gallant Turks in the world?"

Colonel, smiling: "Don't make any more excuses, pray, my remarks were only in return for your joke. Now, about my little girl, I found she was very fond of sweets, and often indulged her taste by presents of the finest I could procure at the pastry cook's; meanwhile, I several times hinted to Mrs. Spooner, the housekeeper, that I suspected someone of tasting the spirits in the cabinet of my sanctum whenever I happened to leave the key in the lock by accident, assuring her that if I could only catch the thief I would take the law into my own hands and birch her bare bottom till it was raw, which she seemed to think would be proper. Having prepared the ground I got some very curious sugar plums made with a most insidious and delightfully intoxicating liqueur concealed inside. I knew little Emma usually had a glass of beer for her lunch, and managed to beckon her into my room directly she had swallowed it one afternoon, and gave her about half a dozen of my special sweets, which she enjoyed immensely as she sat on a footstool at my feet, presently she was drowsy and sleepy, sinking to the floor quite unconscious. Putting the keys in the partially opened door of my cabinet, I then poured about a tea spoonful of rum into her gaping mouth to make her breath smell, and then slipped out unobserved into the grounds where I talked with the gardener for about a quarter of an hour, and then going back to the house by the front door, which Mrs. Spooner opened to me herself. She followed me to my room for the purpose of taking instructions about a proposed party; and we of course discovered the little thief drunk upon the hearth rug before my fire. The mother turned pale with emotion, but I calmly asked her to smell the child's breath to see what she had been tippling, and rang the bell for another of the servants to witness our discovery. Mrs. Spooner could not restrain her tears as she lifted up little Emma, sobbing: "My Gracious! To think of her drinking rum: Oh! Sir, I'll whip her finely for this, leave her to me." "No, indeed, it's far too serious a case for the correction to be left to a tender hearted mother who has evidently ruined her child for want of correction when she has been in fault before; if it had been one of my own servants you know what I intended to do; and now I shall send for a constable and take her before a magistrate, unless you like to leave the punishment to me." Mrs. Spooner was amenable to reason in a moment, but I made her sign a paper confessing the guilt of her child, and asking me to whip her well for the fault, which she signed, crying, and distressed beyond measure. Then the little culprit was put to bed in order to be brought up fresh for punishment the next day. After dinner the ensuing evening I had the whole household in my sanctum; little Emma, all of a glow, was brought in by her mother, her eyes full of tears, and I could see the bursting indignation as I asked her to confess her fault. "Indeed, no, Sir, I never touched the rum or anything except the sweets you gave me, they must have sent me to sleep," she replied, with flushing eyes and crimson face. "Mrs. Spooner," I said, angrily, "bare her naughty bottom immediately, there is nothing will do such an obstinate little thing any good, except this tickler makes her repent that impudent lie," as I whisked my rod through the air. The mother's hands trembled so, and such a deluge of tears rolled down her face, that one of the servants had to assist her in turning up the clothes of the little victim, who kicked and shrieked with all her might; but what a delicious little bottom they exposed, firm, plump, and almost rosy, which I afterwards found out was the effect of a preliminary slapping from her mother's hands. "Ah! No! No!! I won't be whipped. I did not do it, Sir!" she screamed struggling to get away. Whack.... Whack.... fell my birch, each stroke crimsoning her buttocks with a confused lot of red angry looking marks, as I went on lecturing her on her obstinacy, and the awful sin of telling lies to screen her fault, assuring her that I would flay her alive unless she confessed the theft. She was obstinate in the extreme, biting her lips till the blood dripped over her chin, rather than confess she had tasted my rum. Her bottom soon got quite raw, the blood dripping down her lovely white thighs till her stocking were stained, and her shoes were invaded by the dropping claret; at last she fainted, and her mother's distress, as she sobbingly asserted that I had cruelly murdered her darling, was so ludicrous that I had half a mind to order her to be tied up as an accomplice with her daughter. Just then I thought of this salt, and taking it out of a cabinet, where it had been for some time quite forgotten, every one was surprised by its marvellous reviving effects."

Whilst this was being told Julia had been brought round, first opening her eyes, and then sitting up, when a little pinch of the salt was applied by Miss Debrette to her nostrils, and instantly produced such convulsive sneezing that she was thoroughly aroused and heard the conclusion of the lecturer's anecdote.

"Now, Julia," resumed the Colonel, "my lecture is drawing to a close and I dare say you think I have been playing with you in the wolf and lamb style quite long enough; but that is another point for me to make an observation upon. The very fact of accusing your victim of some offence, which she knows herself to be innocent of, adds to your pleasure, it arouses all those blushing indignant looks, and gives you full scope to work upon her obstinate disposition, for they scarcely ever will acknowledge what they know is false, their rage and indignation urge them to die rather than give in, and thus we get the greatest possible enjoyment from the prolonged excitement. Please, step to that post, Miss Ponsonby, which the gentlemen have kindly put up for your benefit."

The black-bearded gentleman takes Julia by the hand with most affectionate solicitude, whispering in her ear as he secures one wrist, "that they have not much more to go through before their final happiness will be crowned," and: "Oh! my dearest Julia, what excess of delight we shall have when you surrender to me all the charms I am now assured you possess!"

She blushes tremendously at this allusion to their marriage, but a sudden painful jerk suspends her by one wrist to a ring high up the post, with her feet quite off the floor, her wrist seems broken, and the anguish, both of body and mind, throws her into renewed fits of hysterical sobbing, as she piteously begs her persecutors to hurry through what they intend to inflict.

Colonel. — "My dear Miss Ponsonby, you ask a most unreasonable thing; my lecture is for your edification as well as the rest of the company; how can you be so absurd as to ask me to spoil the whole effect by bungling hurry? Now I must get those tight fitting drawers off your posteriors; you have both legs and one arm at liberty, and can plunge about to your heart's content at every stroke, and delight us all by the sight of your beautiful motions." Slash…. Slash…. Slash!!!

He is armed with a big hunting whip, and each cut sounds with a sharp crack on the tight fitting drawers fraying and tearing the fabric, and cutting the skin underneath: the poor girl writhes, waving her arm, and kicking her legs about in every possible way, but her struggles only increase the agony by the jerking strain upon her wrist. "Oh! Oh! Oh!!! Ah-r-r-r-re! I am dying now!" she screams, and then sobs in a lower tone: "When will this fearful torture be over! Oh! Let me die now! Kill me! Kill me in mercy!"

Colonel, getting dreadfully excited: "Now, my ladies, watch the beautiful effects of every slashing cut; drink in all the cries, sobs, and groans; look at the tattered drawers, and the delicious virgin blood as it runs all over her person; how the sensation of erotic voluptuousness thrills through my veins at every stroke. I must really kill her!"

His blows search out every unscathed portion of her body; chemise, drawers, and stockings are all cut to ribbons: still the poor victim screams and struggles with extraordinary vigour, sometimes climbing up the post in her agony by entwining it in her legs and arms to relieve the wrist, and then now again falling with all her weight upon the strained joint, as she fails to sustain the exertion or a more fearful cut than usual pulls her down; her bottom is a mass of raw flesh, none of the company utter a word except with bated breath or hot excited whispers, all are in a state of intensely voluptuous excitement as they watch the scene and listen to the slashes of the whip; the victim is now too agonized to scream, her tongue clings to the parched roof of her mouth, and presently the Colonel drops his whip from exhaustion, as the wretched victim swoons again.

Colonel, with a gasp for breath: "Let her down, now for the finishing tableau, we can marry your lordship without the clergyman, now she is unconscious, it will be a delicious treat to see how she feels and thinks of her degradation when she comes round."

They apply the salts again, and pour some cordial down the burning throat; the effect is again magical, the sufferer opens her eyes for a moment, whilst the hands relax their previous clenched position. The ladies at the Colonel's suggestion proceed to act as bridesmaids by arranging Julia on a large mattress on the floor with a pillow under her head and another under the bleeding rump with her legs wide apart offering a most luscious sight to the excited lover who throws off his coat, lets down his trousers, and falling on his knees instantly presents the head of his rampant priapus to Julia's slit, the pouting lips of which are slightly open, and allow her sore clitoris to be seen in its stiffened state. The steed plunges on his impetuous course with a most painful thrust. Julia winces, and the sudden shock thoroughly awakens her to the outrage that is being attempted. She struggles to throw him off, but the ladies hold her down, encouraging his lordship to thrust home and make a woman of her, which he does with such effect as to split through the hymen and crash through every virgin obstacle to his progress; his victim gives a most piercing shriek and almost faints, but Miss Debrette putting her hand underneath applies some of the salt to her wounded clitoris and just inside the lips of her cunny so that the poor girl almost springs with agony to the intense delight of her lover and his friends. He keeps himself well in hand and restrains his own ardour, whilst enjoying all the emotions of the horrified and agonized girl beneath him. The Colonel chaffs and jeers the victim on her lascivious motions, adding to the intensity of her profound disgust and humiliation. Julia screams, sighs, and tries in vain to screen her face from their sight; but her hands are pulled back that they may gloat over the picture of her misery. Miss Debrette seizes a birch and lays on to his lordship's posteriors till she makes him start on the race of love with renewed fury. Julia's feelings too are no longer to be restrained, her bursting heat and the soothing effect of his motions carry her away in spite of herself; she swims in a heaven of delight, her screams and cries change to hysterical sobs of delirious joy, and she spends in ecstasy in response to the drenching shower of love which he shoots for the third time into her still insatiate womb. Every one is entranced with the delightful sight, till at last the Colonel announces that the curtain must fall upon this blissful conclusion to his lecture.

Julia was really married to Lord Flashington as soon as possible, and became one of the most energetic members of the Society of Aristocratic Flagellants.

FINIS

THE

YELLOW ROOM

OR,

ALICE DARVELL'S SUBJECTION

A TALE OF THE BIRCH

BY

M. LE COMTE DU BOULEAU

BIRCHGROVE PRESS

The Yellow Room was first published in 1891, probably by Augustin Brancart, and reprinted c. 1907 by Charles Carrington in Paris. The name of the author, M. Le Comte du Bouleau, is, of course, a pseudonym. Authorship is attributed to an English lawyer, Stanislas Matthew de Rhodès (1857-1932). He is also credited with writing *Gynecocracy* (1893) and *The Petticoat Dominant* (1898). *Gynecocracy* has also been attributed, on circumstantial evidence, to the English psychologist, Henry Havelock Ellis (1859-1939). *The Confessions of Georgina*, an ostensibly Victorian flagellant text, is also attributed to de Rhodès but it is possibly a later, modern, pastiche.

THE

YELLOW ROOM

CONTENTS

"There is nothing, I am convinced by several years' experience, so good for a girl as a thorough good flogging administered upon her bare bottom with an elastic birch, she having been compelled to take off her own drawers herself."

EXTRACT FROM A LETTER OF MRS. B. H***N.

CHAPTER I

SIMPLICITY SHOCKED

"Come in," said Coupeau. "No one will eat you."
—*L'Assommoir*

When the widowed aunt of Miss Alice Darvell, with
whom she had been living for several years in
Yorkshire, died, her residence was transferred to her
nearest relative and guardian's house in Suffolk. And
the change from a small house in a bleak and lonely
part of the West Riding to a baronet's establishment
was hailed with rapture by the handsome and healthy
girl of eighteen. The only, or at any rate, the principal,
advantage gained by her life with her aunt was one
she scarcely appreciated. The life, the bracing air, the
country rambles, and the rigorous punctuality of the
old lady had allowed Miss Darvell to fully develop all
the physical charms which so distinguished her. And
not only that, to the fresh complexion, laughing brown
eyes, and the magnificent contour of her form and of
her limbs was added a distracting air of reckless
ingenuousness, picked up no doubt in her moorland
scampers. But become conscious of her charms, she
sighed for the pomps and vanities of the world. They
were held up to her by her aunt as perils of the
deadliest description—a view regarded by Alice with
skeptical curiosity. Her solitude increased her
imaginative faculty, and the fascination it attached to

balls, parties, and life generally in the world was greater than their charm actually warrants, as Alice subsequently found out. The only disquiet she had experienced arose from a vague longing which was satisfied by none of the small events in her puritanical life. She was modest even to prudishness; had long worn dresses of such a length as to make them remarkable; had never in her life had a low one on; blushed at the mention of an ankle, and would have fainted at the sight of one. The matter of sex was a perpetual puzzle to her, but she was perfectly unembarrassed in her intercourse with men, and quite unconscious of the desire she excited in them. All she knew of her Sir Edward Bosmere of Bosmere Hall was that he was her trustee and guardian; that he was a widower much older than herself, a cousin some degrees removed from her, but that, notwithstanding, she called him "Uncle."

Thither then she went. Sir Edward turned out to be a man of about fifty; very determined in his manner, powerfully built, and of a medium height. But what surprised Alice most was to find herself introduced to a tall, dark girl who looked about two and twenty, as his housekeeper. She was dressed in exquisite fashion, but Alice thought most indecently. Even more shocking, she, too, called Sir Edward, "Uncle."

The first few days were taken up in making acquaintance, but Alice was surprised one morning at breakfast to see Maud grow very pale when told by Sir Edward, that she was to go to the yellow room after breakfast, and that she was to go straight there. This direction was in consequence of some cutlets which were served at the meal being slightly overcooked; and when Alice again saw Maud, she was flushed and excited, and appeared to have been crying her eyes out. In some consternation, she inquired what the yellow room was, and the only reply she obtained was that she would find out soon enough. On the same occasion, when Maud had left the breakfast-room, Sir Edward, who had by that time quite taken in Alice, told her he thought she dressed in a very dowdy fashion, and said he had given directions to their maid to provide a more suitable wardrobe for her. The girl was covered with blushes and confusion when he spoke of her dressing like Maud. Now Maud showed a great deal of leg and of other charms; so Alice tried to pull herself together and reply that she really could do no such thing. Sir Edward looked at her in a very peculiar way, and said he felt sure her present mode of dress hid the loveliest neck and limbs in the world. He went on to ask whether she did not admire Maud's style of dress, and if she had noticed her stockings and drawers.

"I have indeed, uncle; but I could never wear anything like them."

"And why not, pray?"

"I should be so ashamed."

"We will soon cure you of that. We punish prudish young women here by shortening their petticoats. How do you like that idea?"

"Not at all; and I will not have anything of the sort done to me."

"I am afraid, miss, you want a whipping."

"I should like" (defiantly) "to know who would dare such a thing."

Sir Edward again looked at her in a peculiar manner, but said nothing more on the subject. Simply observing that he thought it right that young women should learn how to manage a house before they had one of their own and did not know what to do with it, he said she and Maud were to take the management in turn weekly, and that a week from that day she would have to do so.

"In the meantime, my dear, you had better learn as much as you can from Maud; especially not to let them burn cutlets like these." Saying which, he left the room.

At this point the narrative can best be continued by Alice Darvell herself:

Wed., July 3, 188***.—As soon as uncle had left the breakfast-table, I felt quite disturbed, but on the whole determined to go on as if nothing had happened. A message came a little later by our maid from Maud to say that she could not go out riding as we had arranged. What a terrible woman our "maid" is! Why on earth does uncle have a Scotch-woman of so terrible an aspect for us two girls? She makes you quake if she only looks at me. Well, I made up my mind to go alone; and rode off very soon after.

On my return I met Maud, very red, and looking as though she had been crying dreadfully. She would not tell me what had happened. The rest of the day passed in the usual way. We drove out after lunch, paid some visits, received several at our kettle-drum, dressed for dinner; and while waiting for the gong to sound Maud came to me, and to my horror began talking upon precisely the same subject Sir Edward had been speaking to me about at breakfast.

"Uncle does not approve of your dresses, you little prude, and Janet (the Scotch maid) has another one for you."

"If Janet," said I, "has a dress for me like yours, showing my neck and breasts and back, and my feet, my ankles, my legs—I mean like yours—I declare flatly I won't wear it."

"Don't be a fool, dear. I am mistress this week; you will be next week, as uncle has explained to you, and if you do not get rid of your ridiculous shame you will be soundly punished. You may be thankful if you are only obliged to show your legs up to your knees and your bosom down to your breasts. That is all."

"I do not care. I have never been punished."

"Very well," said Maud; "have your own way. You will soon know better."

When I got down, there were uncle and Maud, three or four young men, and some very handsome women in low dresses, every one; I was the only one in a high dress. Uncle said something to Maud, who whispered to me that I was to go with her. As soon as we got into the hall, she told me I was to be taken to the yellow room and that I was a goose. I asked her, why; she only laughed. Arrived there, she said she was very sorry, but must obey orders. She then strapped my hands firmly behind my back. My struggles were useless in the end, but kept her so long that she said, "I shall take care that you shall have an extra half-dozen for this." I could not think what she meant. It got darker, and still no one came. The yellow room was in an out-of-the-way wing, and I heard the tower clock strike ten. My hands behind me began to hurt, and I began to lose my temper. I wondered how long I was to be kept there, and then who had the right to keep me; and supposed it was called the yellow room because the curtains of the windows, the valances, and the bed-curtains were all yellow damask, and then I wondered what the ottoman, such an enormous one, was doing here, in company with a heavy oak table, a bar swinging from the ceiling, and—what with vexation and impaticncc I wcnt to slccp.

I was awakened at about half-past eleven by the sound of carriages driving off. It was pitch dark and the curtains had been drawn. I know it was about half-past eleven because about half-an-hour later midnight struck. There was a footstep in the corridor, and uncle came in. He said:—

"I am extremely surprised at your insubordination, miss, for which I am about to punish you." What followed I cannot write.

So much for that part of the diary. Later on, by way of penance, as the sequel will show, Miss Alice Darvell was compelled to write out the minutest description of her punishments and her sensations and secret thoughts.

What happened was this: Sir Edward Bosmere at once informed Alice that he would have no more prudish nonsense; that he was going to strip her and flog her soundly, when he had first obtained a promise from her to take off her own drawers—a very important humiliation to which to subject a proud young beauty. She protested in the most vehement manner.

"He had no right to whip her; she would not be whipped by any man or anyone else; he was at once to undo her hands; being kept all the evening in that room without any dinner was quite punishment enough; she did not know why she had been punished; she would not wear horrid dresses which only served to make nakedness conspicuous; and if she was going to be treated in this way, she would go away tomorrow." "As to promising to take off her own drawers, and before him, he must be mad to think of such a thing, and she would die first."

She looked lovely in her fury, and an alteration in the surface of Sir Edward's trousers showed his appreciation of her beauty. He longed to see her naked and all her charms revealed.

"I will not dispute with you, you saucy miss, and as your face is too pretty to slap; I will settle accounts with your bottom—yes, your bottom, and a pretty plump white bottom I have no doubt it is. I can promise you, however, it won't be white long. Now lie across that ottoman on your face. What? You won't? Well, across my knee will do as well, and perhaps better."

Putting his arm round her waist, he dragged the girl with him to the sofa, telling her that her shrieks and struggles in that heavily curtained and thickly carpeted room were of no avail; that even if they were heard no one would pay attention to them, and that the only result would be, if she went on, to double her punishment. He did not, however, at that moment wish to do more than examine the charms that were so jealously concealed, the magnificence of which might be easily guessed from the little that did appear of her figure. He walked her to the sofa and sat down upon it, still holding her by the waist, and then, putting her between his legs, pulled her down across his left one. Her power of resistance was very much lessened by her hands being strapped behind her, but still she managed to slide down upon her knees in front of him instead of being laid across his lap. He then held her tightly between his knees and proceeded to unfasten the neck of her dress, and as the buttons were at the back he was obliged to put his arms round her and draw her so close that he felt her warm pressure upon him. The passion he felt was intensified, and the girl then, for the first time, seemed in a hazy sort of wonder as to whether the treatment she was undergoing was altogether unpleasant, which occupied her to such an extent that she ceased her useless resistance. At length the buttons were all undone to the waist. The dress was pulled down in front as far as the strapped-back arms would allow; sufficient, however, to disclose a neck as white as snow and the upper surfaces of two swelling, firm globes. Sir Edward immediately, placing his left arm under his victim's armpit and round her shoulders, drew her closer to him, spreading his legs wider, and notwithstanding her pretty cries to him to desist, inserted his right hand in her bosom. At last, succeeding in loosening her corset, he was able to caress the scarlet centre of the lovely, palpitating breast whose owner lay in most bewitching disorder in his lap. Her hair had partly fallen; her bosom was exposed by the dress three parts down and the loose corset—her eyes swam, and her colour was heightened.

"Oh, stop! uncle; oh, do, do, do stop! I never felt like this before. Whatever will become of me? I cannot bear the sensation. You have no business to pull me about so."

"Do you not like the sensation, Alice?" asked he, stooping and putting his face into her bosom, "and being kissed like this, and this, and this? And is not this nice?"—taking her red teat between his lips and gently playing with it with his tongue.

"Oh! uncle! whatever are you doing to me?" said the girl, flushing crimson all over, and her eyes opening wide with amazement, while her knees fell wider apart, as she herself fell slightly back upon his right knee.

"Is it nice? Do you like it? Does it give you sensations anywhere else?" asked he, glancing at her waist—and then, a moment after, putting his hand down outside her dress, said, "here, for instance?"

Still a deeper blush of crimson shame, but there was a gleam of rapture after the momentary pressure, followed by the exclamation: "How dare you?"

"How dare I, miss? We shall see. Now you will please lie on your face across my knee. You can rest on the sofa."

"Oh, I suppose"—with some disappointment in the tone—"that you are now going to button up my dress."

"Am I?"

"Then what are you going to do?"

"Make you obey me, and without any more resistance, or you shall have double punishment. Lie down at once, miss."

"Oh, uncle, don't look at my legs! Oh, do not, do not strip me. Oh, if I am to be whipped, whip my hands or shoulders; not there."

"You are a very naughty, obstinate girl, with very much too much prudishness about you. But when you yourself have been forced to expose all you possess in the most unconcealed manner, and have been kept some days in short frocks with no drawers, there will no doubt be an improvement. And, as I said before, I shall flog your bare bottom soundly, Miss Alice; and pretty often if you do not mend. Lash your arms and shoulders, indeed. I shall lash your legs and thighs. Lie down this instant."

The poor girl, seeing resistance useless, said nothing; but the arm put round her back soon cured her inaction. She lay across her uncle's left leg and under his left arm, which he had well round her waist.

"Now," said he, tightening his grasp, "we shall see what we have all along so carefully hidden; eh, miss?" pulling up her dress behind, despite her struggles and reiterated prayers to him to desist.

"No use struggling, miss," he went on, slipping his hand up her legs and proceeding at once to that organ in front which women delights to have touched.

"Oh, uncle! Oh, leave off. How dare you? How dare you outrage me like this? Oh! Take your hand away! Oh! Oh! Oh!"

"So you are a little wet," feeling the hairs moistened by the voluptuous sensations he had caused her by caressing her breasts; "and you hoped that no one would know, no doubt. Now just let me stroke these legs. What a nice" (turning the robe above her waist) "fine pair they are; and" (opening the drawers) "what a pretty, what a perfectly lovely bottom! What a crime to hide it from me. However, you will make amends for that by taking your drawers off presently."

"Never! Never while I live! You monster! You wretch! If ever I get out of this room alive, I will expose you!"

"My dear, let me try a little gentle persuasion, a novel sensation. If that does not suffice, I can find some more striking argument."

And, again pressing her down upon him, he slipped his hand up, and putting his finger in her virgin orifice in front, he placed his thumb in the rear. Feeling his finger first, she jerked herself upwards, upon which in went his thumb; then, with a little scream, again bouncing forwards, his finger slid in as far as her maidenhead would admit—her hands were all the time still tied. He kept up a severe use of both his finger and thumb for some moments, and she was unable to contain herself, and ultimately obliged to abandon herself to the sensations he provoked. Her legs were stretched out and wide apart; her bottom rose and fell regularly; her lovely neck and shoulders, which were still exposed to his sight, increased his rapture and her dismay; and at last, when the crisis had arrived— pretty nearly at the same moment did it overtake them both—she lay panting and sobbing, almost dead with shame; but for that time subdued.

"Well, dear, how do you like your new experience?"

"Oh, uncle, it is awful, simply awful! I am beside myself."

"When you have rested a moment, will you stand up and take off your drawers before me?"

No answer.

"Answer directly, miss."

"No, I won't! I won't, and you shall not."

Getting up, he went to a chest of drawers, and,

opening one, took out a riding-whip. Silently, and notwithstanding her violent resistance, he again got the refractory girl over his knee, with his arm round her, her dress up, and her bottom as bare as her drawers would admit. Across the linen and the bare part he gave her a vigorous cut, making the whip whistle through the air. It fell, leaving a livid mark across the delicate white flesh, and caused a yell of pain. Again he raised it and brought it down—another yell and desperate contortions.

"Oh, uncle, don't! Oh! no more! no more! Oh! I can't bear it. I will be good. I will obey."

Sir Edward paid no attention, and raising the whip, made it whistle a third time through the air. A more piercing shriek.

"It is not enough for you to promise to obey; you must be punished, and cured of your obstinacy. And you called me a wretch and monster"—swish—swish—swish.

"Oh! oh! oh! oh! oh! oh! oh! don't! oh, don't! Oh, you are not! I say you are not anything but what—oh! oh! put down that whip. Oh! please, dear uncle! You are not a wretch! or monster! I was very naughty to call you so, and I liked what you did to me, only was ashamed to say it. I will take my drawers off before you if you like! I will do *anything*, only don't whip me any more."

"You shall have your dozen, miss"—swish. "So you liked my tickling your clitoris, did you, better than"—swish—"tickling your bottom with this whip, eh?"—swish—swish. "You will expose me if you escape alive, will you?"—swish—swish.

"Oh, stop, stop! You have given me thirteen. For heaven's sake, stop!"

"I have given you a baker's dozen, and"—swish—"there is another because you complained."

Sir Edward was carried away by the passions excited by punishing this lovely girl, and her yell as the whip again cut into her delicate flesh, he did not hear, so beside himself was he. Still holding her, he asked the sobbing girl whether she would be good.

"Yes. Indeed, indeed I will."

"There is a very satisfactory magic in this wand. Now, if I unfasten your hands, will you stand up and take your drawers off so that I may birch your bottom for refusing to wear a proper evening dress?"

"Oh, uncle, you have whipped me once, and punished me severely, too, by what you did to me. Why should I be put to more shame?"

"Shame! Nonsense. You should be proud of your charms and glad to show them. What I did should give you pleasure. Anyhow, will you take off your drawers?"

"Oh!" (flushing and in despair) "however can I? I should have to lift my dress quite up, and I should be all exposed. Besides, it is so humiliating."

"Precisely you yourself must bare all your hidden fascinations. And the humiliation is to chastise your prudishness. You must do it. You had much better be a good, obedient girl, as you promised you would be just now."

"Very well. I will then."

"That is a good girl. You shall have a kiss for reward," and, putting his lips on her beautiful mouth, Sir Edward gave her a long and thrilling kiss, and inserted his tongue until it came into contact with hers.

"What a delicious kiss," she said, shuddering with delight; and coyly added: "I shall not so much mind taking off my—my—my drawers" (in a hushed tone, her eyes averted from him) "*now.*"

"That is right, dear. Now let me undo your hands. There. Now stand before that mirror and let me arrange the light so that it may fall full upon you. Now I shall sit here."

Miss Alice Darvell walked over to the mirror in a graceful and stately fashion, and started as she saw herself. She turned round and looked shyly at her master, but said nothing. Stooping down, she gathered up her gown and petticoats in her arms and slowly lifted them to her waist. The act revealed a slender and graceful pair of ankles and calves, but the knees were hidden by the garment she was about to remove. After fumbling with the buttons about her waist—they increased her confusion by not readily unbuttoning, at which she, in a charming little rage, stamped angrily once or twice—the drawers tumble down.

"Keep up your petticoats," cried Sir Edward, "and step out of your drawers. Keep them up," said he, rising, "until I tell you you may let them down. What lovely thighs! What splendid hips! What a lovely, soft, round bottom! Look at it, Alice, in the glass."

"Oh," she said, simply," "I am so glad you think so. I have never looked at myself before."

At which he laughed, and stroked the satin skin with his hand, rubbing her limbs in front and behind and all over her bottom, until at last, when he had gradually stroked her all the way up, he put his hand between the cheeks of her back right through to her cunt, which, and the passage also, he kept gently stroking for some minutes, while she rested against him, uttering inarticulate sounds of delight.

"There," he said at length, "that will do for to-night. You may let your clothes down now. It is so late that the birching shall be postponed until the morning."

"May I take my drawers with me?"

"No, my dear; it will be some time before I shall allow you to wear them again."

"Oh, uncle!"

"Not as long as you are a maiden," added he, significantly.

"Oh, that will be years."

"Will it?" he inquired, innocently.

"Come," he went on, "I will take you to your room. You will in the future occupy that one to which I am now going to take you, and not your old one."

"Why, uncle? All my things are in the old one."

"That does not matter, my dear. I must keep you under my eye until you are reduced to abject submission."

The room to which he took her was cheery and warm. Although the month was July, a fire had been lighted and had evidently been recently stirred. And on a small table near the hearth stood a biscuit box and a small bottle of Dry Monopole. Alice would have preferred a sweeter wine, but was told that this was better for her. It was quite plain that either uncle had told someone the precise hour at which he would bring her to the room, or that someone had been watching, for the wine was still frothing in the glass, and therefore must have been poured out the very moment before she entered. Terrible thought—Could anyone have been watching *her* and have seen her nakedness? Her uncle could not have known at what hour he would take her there. She was for an instant paralyzed at the notion, but the next moment, accidentally catching sight of a bare breast and arm, it caused her a certain voluptuous thrill to think she had been seen by someone besides Sir Edward. As she slowly undressed herself, her uncle having gone off and shut the door behind him, it struck her that she would herself, for her own satisfaction, have a peep at all she had been compelled to expose to him. She blushed at her own resolution, and commenced to feel what Miss Rosa Broughton describes as delightfully immoral, first taught her by her uncle's hands, and of which all her lifetime until then she had been wholly ignorant, although she had had at times a conviction that some such pleasure exists. She stood before one of the large glasses with several of which her room was furnished, and having let down her wealth of brown hair and divested herself of all but a single garment, she allowed that—her chemise—to slip off her shoulders and arms, and for an instant only gazed at herself in the glass. For an instant only, for, overcome by a flood of shame at her nakedness and at the sense of it, she hurriedly averted her eyes and looked about for her nightdress. That she could not find; and she then recollected that the room was not the same she had previously used, and she supposed they must have forgotten to bring her things. No; here was her dressing-gown. She would put it on and go to her old room for her night dress.

She went to the door, and to her utter amazement, found that there was no handle inside. She was a prisoner. She looked about, but there was no other door anywhere to be seen.

"Very well," she said to herself; "I shall have to sleep in my chemise."

Taking off her dressing-gown when she was again naked to put on the chemise again made her feel immodest, and as it was cut low in the neck and left her arms bare, she felt more immodest still when she had got it on—a sensation renewed on several occasions when she awoke during the night and was reminded by her bare arms of her plight and of what she had undergone—and was to undergo later in the morning.

Before she got into bed she looked about for the article ladies generally use. There was nothing of the kind in the room, and there was no bell. Then it struck her that the deprivation of her nightdress and of the utensil referred to must have been done deliberately by Sir Edward, and the idea that he had thought of such things so intimately connected with her person gave her a fresh delightful glow of sensuality as she plunged into the cold, silky, linen sheets. The necessary effort to retain her urine, the sense that she was being punished by being made to retain it, and the knowledge that her uncle knew all about it and was so punishing her, excited her to such an extent that she went to bed a very naughty girl indeed.

CHAPTER II

INITIATION

"Don't be afraid; a little bleeding does 'em good."
—*L'Assommoir*

Awakening next morning about nine o'clock, she caught herself wondering what the whipping would be like, and how it would be administered, and was filled with a delightful sense of shame when she recollected the part of her body that would receive the castigation and she imagined the exposure it would inevitably entail. The thought or anticipation of this did not disturb her much. She even contemplated with pleasure the exposure there would be of her legs and thighs, and that which she did not name to herself, considering the word immodest; but she did trust that her uncle would not flog her very severely.

As she lay thus occupied with these thoughts, there was a tap at the door, and Janet came in with a cup of tea and some bread-and-butter and the announcement—

"You have just an hour for dressing, miss, for breakfast will be served at half-past ten in the blue sitting-room—the one which overlooks the park. Miss Maud will come to show you where it is."

"Thank you, Janet," said Alice, keeping herself carefully covered. "There are several things I want from my old room—linen and a dress. Will you please bring them?"

"Yes, miss. I have the clothes you are to wear all ready, and will bring them to you."

"What do you mean, Janet? I should like to choose my own dress."

Janet did not reply. She grimly thought she would leave the girl to find out for herself.

She returned presently with an armful of clothing, which she deposited on a sofa.

In the meantime Alice had jumped up and donned the dressing-gown. She then again found it necessary to look about for that piece of furniture which is a feature in most bedrooms, but could not find it anywhere. She did not know, however, how to mention the matter to Janet, and while she was wondering how to accomplish it that amiable domestic had left the room. Alice had told her to return in about half an hour to do her hair, and the reply was that her hair was not to be done up that morning—a circumstance which, recalling what was before her, made her blush deeply. Then Janet departed, shutting the door, which only opened from the outside. Alice, consoling herself with the reflection that she could wait at any rate until she was on the way to breakfast, proceeded to wash. In the wall, close to the wash-hand-stand, was a black marble knob, with the word "Bath" upon it in gold letters. It was exactly what she wanted at the moment. Putting her hand upon it, she happened to press slightly, when the panel slid aside and showed a marble-floored room surrounded by looking-glasses, with several large slabs of cork for standing on, and a large bath of green Irish marble in the centre. Proceeding to it, she found that the same plan filled the bath with water as opened the room itself. She soon ascertained that not only was the water perfumed, but deliciously softened. The champagne and the tea made her wish again that she could have got rid of the water she herself contained, but she could not make out how the water ran away or was made to run away from the bath—so that little idea was knocked on the head. While bathing, she caught sight of herself continually in the glasses about her, and fell in love with her round, plump limbs and frame, and wondered why she had never done so before. She also noticed with indignation the red marks across her bottom made by the cruel whip that night, and shuddered as she dried herself with the deliciously woolly and warmed towels, and re-membered that she had a flogging to undergo. She came, however, to the conclusion that her dis-obedience deserved punishment; and felt naughty, as she confessed to herself that she "really deserved to be whipped for it."

Hardly had she so determined than she found her obedience again put to the test. Proceeding to dress, she found the clothes brought far worse than the dress she had refused to wear the evening before. They were fit for a girl of ten, and, indeed, unfit for even her. The chemise was abominably low behind and before, the petticoats were quite short. So was the dress. And the petticoats were so starched that instead of hiding her limbs they would display them. And there were no drawers. What was she to do? Sir Edward was rigid in exacting punctuality at meals and generally. If she waited till Maud came she would be too late, and probably receive a worse flogging; besides, in all probability, Maud would only again laugh at her. So, a little indignantly, she dressed herself in the white silk stockings, which reached just half-way up her thigh, tied them with the rose-coloured garters above her knee; put on the patent leather low-cut shoes, the black and yellow corset, and the white frock with a rose-coloured sash. She tied her hair with a ribbon of the same colour, and then looked at herself. She looked like a great, overgrown schoolgirl, but, she could not help owning to herself, a very lovely one. Her arms were bare, and the frock was so low that she noticed with horror it only just concealed her red teats, looking at her from straight in front, but that if you looked down from her shoulder they were quite visible. And the dress stopped at her knees; no effort could make it longer. And the petticoats would make it stick out so. The only comfort was her hair, which did help to hide her naked back. Dressed at last, but feeling worse than naked, she sat down to wait for Maud, and, to her horror, noticed in a glass opposite that the dress stuck out to such an extent that not only could her leg be seen to the top of the stocking, but that the rosy flesh beyond was quite visible; and after a trial or two she discovered that if she was not very careful how she sat, not only would the whole of both legs be displayed, but her cunt also. She wondered however she could go about, and whether she would have to; and at last the costume so excited her passions that she was compelled to walk up and down, and became so naughty that she did not know how to contain herself or the water she had been unable to get rid of. While fidgetting about the room in this state of agitation, Maud entered, and immediately exclaimed, in the most disingenuous manner:—

"How perfectly lovely you are, Alice, with that blush-rose flush! What a splendid bust! Good gracious! do let me look at them. What lovely straight beautifully-shaped legs" (catching hold of the skirt of the frock). "Oh, do let me see—"

"Oh! don't, Maud! Don't!"

"Very well, dear. But you have not done up your hair. That won't do."

"Janet told me I was not to."

"Yes; I know. But that was a mistake. It hides too much."

"That is just why I like it down."

"And just why I do not, dear. You must let me roll it up for you so that your back and nuque and shoulders may be fully shown. There; now you look a perfect darling. I thought I should find you quite cured of anxiety to hide any charm. Do you not wish now you had take my advice?"

"Yes."

"But," she went on, "it is not of much consequence; for if you had not rebelled, some other excuse would have been made for punishing you."

"Indeed?"

"Yes; and you deserved it, Alice."

As Alice had herself come to this conclusion, and felt her bare legs, she only blushed, and said:—

"Oh, Maud, do you know I have no drawers on; and that when I sit down my legs and all show? Shall I have to go about in this dress? and how long shall I have to wear it?"

"That depends upon how you take your punishment. While you wear it you will certainly have to go about in the house and grounds with it. I suppose you wish you had drawers on?"

"Indeed you may suppose so. Oh, Maud, however can I—"

"We must be going, Alice, or we shall be late."

"Oh, Maud, do tell me, does uncle whip very hard?"

"I should have thought," and Maud's eyes flashed, "you could have answered that question yourself."

"Yes. He hurt me dreadfully with the riding-whip. Have you been birched?"

"Yes. I have."

"Was it very bad?"

"In a few hours you will be able to judge for yourself."

"How does he birch?"

"Here," said Maud, slyly putting her hand under Alice's petticoats upon her bare bottom.

"Oh, don't, Maud."

"Silly child, you should be obliged to me for the sensation. Do come along to breakfast."

"Oh, Maud, there is something I want to ask you;

but how to do it I do not know. Perhaps" (with a deep blush) "the best way is to say they have forgotten to put something in my room."

"I know very well what you mean, Alice. You mean you have no po; and you want to pea. All I can say is that I hope you do not want to very badly, because it is not at all likely that you will be allowed to do so until after your flogging. But, of course, you can ask uncle."

"However could I ask him?" replied Alice, aghast and pale at the notion and the prospect of what she would have to endure. "Does he know?" remembering her thought of the night.

"Yes. Of course he knows; and he does it to punish you, and to help to make you feel naughty. Do you feel naughty, dear?" asked Maud, and, again putting her hand under Alice's petticoats, she began tickling her clitoris.

"Oh, don't! Maud. Oh, pray don't! Oh, you will make me wet myself if you do. Oh, can't you let me go to your room?"

"My dear girl, if I were to let you pea without permission, I should probably be forbidden to do so oftener than twice in the twenty-four hours for a week or a fortnight. And I advise you to say nothing about it to uncle, for if he finds out that you want to very badly, he will probably make you wait another hour. It is a very favourite punishment of his."

"Why?"

"Oh, I don't know; except that it is a severe one. And it is awfully humiliating to a girl to have to ask; but it certainly makes one feel naughty."

"Yes; it does. Do you know, I was nearly doing it in the bath?"

"Lucky for you that you did not. It would certainly have been found out, and you would have caught it. But, Alice, why do you say 'doing it' instead of 'peaing'? When you ask you will have to use plain language."

"Oh, Maud!"

"Yes; and very likely have to do it before uncle. If he finds out you squirm about saying things and calling them by their names, he will make you say the most outrageous things, and write them also. But there is half-past ten chiming. Come along."

When they got to the blue room—on the way to which they passed, to Alice's intense consternation, several servants who gazed immoveably at her—they found Sir Edward there in a velvet coat and kilt. He greeted them cheerily. The view across the park, in the glades of which the fallow deer could be seen grazing, was, lovely; the sunshine was flooding the room, and the soft, warm summer air wafted in the perfume of the flowers from the beds below (the blue room was on the bedroom floor) through the windows, which were thrown wide open. Alice was so struck by the view that she for a moment forgot to notice how her uncle was gazing at her, until she felt the air on her legs, and it provoked a consciousness at which she blushed.

"How do you like your frock, my dear? It becomes you admirably."

"Does it, uncle?" Looking coyly at him. "I am glad you like it."

"I am glad to see you are a sensible girl after all. We shall make something of you."

"How long am I to wear it, uncle?"

"For a week."

"For a fortnight," struck in Maud, maliciously. "She is to be mistress next week."

Maud knew very well she would find it much worse to be dressed like that when giving orders, and that her orders would not be so well attended to. She revelled in the notion of getting Alice soundly punished.

Sir Edward noticed with a gleam of amusement how fidgetty Alice became towards the end of the meal, and Maud smiled gently to herself. Alice thought that after breakfast she would have a chance. She was disappointed. Sir Edward then said, in a severe tone: "I think, Miss Alice, we have a little business to settle together. Your disobedience cannot be overlooked. You must come with me. Your short skirts will punish your prudishness, but the birch is the best corrector of a bold, disobedient girl's bottom." She grew quite pale, and trembled all over, both with fright and at being spoken to so before Maud, who, reposing calmly in her chair, was steadily gazing at her.

She had got up. When her uncle had finished speaking, he came up to her and took hold of her left ear with his right hand, and saying, "Come along, miss, to be flogged," marched her off to the yellow room.

There, to her consternation, she saw straps and pillows on the oak table. In a perfect fright, she said: "Oh, pray do not strap me up, uncle; pray do not. I will submit."

"Undress yourself," he said, having closed the door; "leave on your stockings only."

"Oh, uncle!"

"You had better obey, miss, or you shall have a double dose. Take off your frock this instant."

"Now your petticoat bodice."

"Now your petticoats. Now your corset and chemise. Now, my proud young beauty, how do you feel?"

He had not seen her to such advantage the evening before. She had then had her long dress on the whole time, and while punishing her he had only uncovered a small portion of her legs. It is true she afterwards had been made to take off her drawers; but the skirt and petticoats gathered about her hips had still concealed much. Now she was naked from the crown of her head to her rose coloured garters. Burning with shame, she put her hands up to her face, and remained standing and silent, while Sir Edward feasted his eyes upon the contemplation of every beautiful curve of the lovely little head poised so beautifully upon a perfect throat; of the dimpled back and beautifully rounded shoulders; of the arms; of the breasts and hips and thighs. It was the most lovely girl he had seen, he said to himself, and then, seating himself, he added aloud:—

"Come here, miss. Kneel down: there, between my knees; clasp your hands, and say after me:—

"Uncle, I have been."

"Uncle, I have been."

"A naughty, disobedient girl,"

"A naughty, disobedient girl."

"And deserve to be soundly birched."

"And deserve to be soundly birched."

"Please, therefore,"

"Please, therefore,"

"Strap me down"

"Oh, no! oh, no! Oh, please don't strap me down!"

"Say what I tell you at once, miss, or it will be worse for you."

"Strap me down"

"To the table,"

"Oh! oh! oh! To the table,"

"With my legs well apart,"

"Oh, dear! I can't. With—with—I can't—with my— oh, uncle!"

"An extra half-dozen for this."

"Oh, uncle!"

"Say at once: With my legs well apart."

"With my—my—oh!—legs" (and she shuddered

deliciously and blushed bewilderingly) "well apart."

"And give me"

"And give me"

"Please,"

"Please,"

"Four and a half dozen"

"Oh, uncle! please not so much!" (recollecting the baker's dozen with the riding-whip.)

"You will have more if you do not say it at once."

"Four and a half dozen"

"On my bare bottom."

"Oh! that!—my—I can never say—"

"You must."

"My bare—"

"You had better say it. Stop; I will improve it. You must say: On my girl's bare bottom."

"Oh, uncle!" she said, looking at him; and seeing his eyes gloating upon her and devouring her beauty, and the lust and fire in them, she immediately turned hers away.

"Now, Alice, 'On my girl's bare bottom.'"

"On my girl's bare bottom."

He moved as he said this, and Alice noticed he adjusted some thing under his kilt.

"Well laid on."

"Well laid on."

"Yes; I will, my dear. I will warm your bottom for you as well as ever any girl ever had her bottom warmed. I will set it on fire for you. You will curse the moment you were disobedient. I will cure you of disobedience and all your silly nonsense. Come along to the table. There, stand at that end"—Alice began to sob—"put the cushion before you, so. Now lie over it, right down on the table. No resistance" (as he fixed the strap round her shoulders she made a slight attempt at remonstrance). The strap went round her and the table, and when once it was buckled she could not, of course, get up. He then buckled on two wristlets, and with two other straps fastened her wrists to the right and left legs of the table; then another broad strap was put round the table and the small of her back. This was pretty tight, as were also those that at the knees and ankles fastened her legs, wide apart, to the legs of the table. She was like a spread eagle, and her bottom, the tender skin between its cheeks, her cunt, and her legs were most completely exposed.

"Now, my dear, you will remain in that position half an hour and contemplate your offences, and then you shall have as sound a flogging as I ever gave a girl."

"Oh, uncle, before you flog me, do let me do something. Maud told me I should have to tell you, but I do not know how to. I will come back directly and be strapped down again if you will only let me. And, oh! please do not leave me in this dreadful position for half an hour."

"You must say what it is that you want."

"Oh, uncle"—feeling it was neck or nothing—"do let me go and pea before I am flogged. I want to, oh, so dreadfully. I have not been able to all the morning, nor all night."

"So you want to very dreadfully, do you, miss?" and going up to her he put his hand between her legs from behind, and severely tickled the opening through which the stream was burning to rush. It was all that Alice could do to retain it.

"Oh, don't! Oh! If you do I shall wet myself. I shall not be able to help it. Oh, uncle, pray, pray don't! Oh, pray let me go!"

"No, miss, I certainly shall not. It is a part of your punishment. There was an unnatural coldness about these parts of yours which this will help to warm up. Have you not felt more naughty since you have had all that hot water inside you?"

"Yes; I have."

"And you are beginning to see how ridiculous prudishness is. Now, just you think about your conduct and your disobedience until I return to whip you, and remember you owe your present shameful position to them."

Saying this, Sir Edward left the room. Poor Alice, left to herself, all naked save for her stockings; her arms stretched out above her head and tightly strapped; her legs divided and fastened wide apart; the most secret portions of her frame made the most conspicuous in order that they might be punished by a man—did feel her position acutely. She considered it and felt it to be most shameful. Her cheeks burned with a hot, red glow. But all concealment was absolutely impossible; the haughty beauty felt herself prostrate before and at the mercy of her master, and experienced again an exquisite sensual thrill at the thought that she really deserved to have her bottom whipped by her uncle.

Presently Maud came into the room in a low-necked dress, with a large bouquet.

"Well, Alice," she said, "I hope you enjoy your position and the prospect before you."

"Oh, Maud; go away. I can't bear you to see me in this position. I won't be punished before you."

"Silly goose! Young ladies strapped down naked, and stretched out for punishment like spread eagles, are not entitled to say shall or shan't. What a lovely skin and back, Alice. Alas! before long that pretty, plump, white bottom will present a very altered appearance. How many are you to have?"

"I was made to ask for four dozen and a half, well laid on."

"And you may depend upon it, you will have them,

my dear, most mercilessly laid on"—stroking her legs and thighs, which caused Alice to catch her breath and to coo in a murmuring way from the pleasure Maud's hand gave her. Maud asked her whether she had tried to induce her uncle to let her go somewhere.

"Yes," replied Alice; "I did. But he would not."

"And I suppose you want to very badly," went on Maud, maliciously placing her fingers on the very spot.

"Yes; I do. Oh, don't, Maud, or you'll make me!"

"Now mind, Alice, whatever you do, hold out till your birching is over. If you do not I warn you that you will catch it."

"I think it is a very, very cruel, horrid punishment," said Alice, whimpering.

"It is severe, I know, and it is far better not to be prudish than to incur it. But here comes uncle."

"Now, you bold, disobedient girl, I hope you feel ashamed of yourself," said Sir Edward, entering the room and shutting the door.

"Maud will witness your punishment as a warning to her what she will receive if she is disobedient."

Going up to the wardrobe, he selected three well-pickled birches, which had evidently never been used, for there were numbers of buds on them. They were elastic and well spread, and made a most ominous switching sound as, one by one, Sir Edward switched them through the air at which Alice shuddered and Maud's eyes gleamed.

"Oh, pray, pray, uncle, do not be very severe. Remember it is almost my first whipping. It is awful!"

Maud had changed the dress she had worn at breakfast and, as already mentioned, now had on one cut very low in the body; her arms were bare and her skirts short. Between her breasts was placed a bouquet of roses.

"Hold these," said Sir Edward, giving her the rods.

He then put his left arm round Alice, and said: "Now, you saucy, disobedient miss, your bottom will expiate your offences, and by way of preface"—smack, smack with his right hand, smack, smack, smack.

"Ah, it is already becoming a little rosy."

"Oh, uncle! Oh, how you hurt! Oh, how your hand stings! Oh! oh! oh!"

"Yes. A bold girl's bottom must be well stung. It teaches her obedience and submission"—smack— "what a lovely, soft bottom!"—smack, smack, smack.

Maud's eyes gleamed and her face flustered, as Alice, wriggling about as much as the straps allowed, cried softly to herself. When her uncle had warmed her sufficiently, he removed his arm and moved about two feet away from the girl, whose confusion at the invasion of her charms by the rough hand of a man increased her loveliness tenfold. Maud held one birch in her right hand. She, too, looked divine. Her dark eyes flashing, her lovely bosom heaving, she handed it, retaining the other two in her left hand, to her uncle. Alice could not see that as she gave him the birch, as soon as her hand was free she slipped it under her uncle's kilt from the back, and the instant increase of his passion and excitement left no doubt as to the use she was making of it. Sir Edward stood at the left side of his refractory ward. He drew the birch, lecturing her as he did so, three or four times upwards and downwards from back to front and from front to back between the cheeks of the girl's bottom, producing a voluptuous movement of the lovely thighs and little exclamations of delight.

"Oh! oh! oh! don't do that! Oh! oh! how dreadful! Oh, please, uncle!" trying to turn found, which, of course, the straps prevented. He next proceeded to birch her gently all over, the strokes increasing in vigour, but being always confined to the bottom.

"Oh, uncle, you hurt! Oh! how the horrid thing stings! Oh! it is worse than your hand! Oh! stop! Have I not had enough?"

"We will begin now, miss," said he, having given her a cut severe enough to provoke a slight cry of real pain; "and Maud will count."

Lifting up the rod at right angles to the table on which she was bound down, he brought it down with a tremendous swish through the air across the upper parts of her hips.

"One," said the mellow voice of Maud—her right hand and a portion of her arm hidden under her uncle's kilt, the movements of its muscles under the delicate skin and the wriggles of the Baronet showing that Maud had hold of and was kneading a sensitive portion of his frame. The bottom grew crimson where the stroke had fallen, and the culprit emitted a yell and gasped for breath. With the regularity of a steamhammer, he again raised the rod well above his shoulder, and again making it whistle through the air, he again gave her a very severe stroke.

"Two," said Maud quietly.

A shriek. "Oh! stop! Oh! stop! Oh! *stop!*"

Swish. "Three," calmly observed Maud.

"Oh! you will kill me. Oh! I can't—I can't—"

Swish. "Four, uncle."

"Oh, ah! Oh, I can't bear it! Oh, I will be good! Oh, Maud, ask him to stop—"

Swish. "Five"

Maud had given her uncle an extra pull when Alice had appealed to her, and this stroke was harder in consequence. Spots of blood began to appear where the ends of the birch and its buds fell, especially on the outside of the off thigh. The yell which followed number five was more piercing, and choking sobs ensued; but Sir Edward, merely observing that she would run a very good chance of extra punishment if she made so much noise, without heeding her tears or contortions or choking, mercilessly and relentlessly gave her six, seven, eight, and nine, each being counted by Maud's clear gentle voice.

"Now, miss, that you have had one-sixth of your punishment—"

"One-sixth! Oh! oh! oh! I can't bear more! Oh, I can't bear more! Oh, let me off! You will kill me! Oh, let me off! I will—I will I *will* indeed be good—"

"I suppose you begin to regret your disobedience."

"Oh, don't punish me any more," cried the girl, wriggling and struggling to get free—of course ineffectually, but looking perfectly lovely in her pain.

"Yes! You must receive the whole number. It is not enough to promise to obey now; you should have thought of this before. You are now having your bottom punished, not only to make you better in future, but for your past offences."

And Sir Edward walked round to the right side of his niece, and there, in the same place, but from right to left, gave her nine very severe cuts. Alice yelled and screamed and roared and rolled about as much as she possibly could, perfectly reckless as to what she showed.

The next nine were given lengthwise between her legs. Her bottom being well up, and the legs well apart, the strokes fell upon the tender skin between them, and the long, lithe ends of the rod curled round her cunt, causing her excruciating agony.

"There is nothing like a good birching for a girl." Swish.

"One," said Maud, moving voluptuously.

"Oh! oh! yah! Oh! my bottom! Oh! my legs! Oh! how it hurts! Oh! oh! oh!"

"They are all the better for the pain!" Swish.

"Two," said Maud.

"Oh! oh! oh! Oh, don't strike me there!" as the birch curled round her cunt.

"And the exposure. I do not think you will disobey." Swish.

"Three," said Maud, apparently beside herself, her eyes swimming.

"Oh! oh! oh! yah! Oh! I shall die! I shall *faint*! Oh! dear uncle! I will—please forgive me—I will never disobey. I will do anything; ANYTHING; ANYTHING!"

"I daresay you will, miss; but I shall not let you off;"—swish—"there's another for your cunt."

"Four," said Maud.

"Oh! Oh! not there! Oh! I am beside myself! I shall go mad! I shall *die* or go *mad*!"

"You will not do anything of the sort, and you must bear your punishment." Swish.

"Five," counted Maud.

The cries gradually lessened, and the culprit seemed to become entranced, whereupon the uncle, at whom Maud looked significantly, directed the remaining four strokes to the insides of the thighs, leaving the palpitating red rose between them free from further blows, for the present.

Alice's moans were then succeeded by piercing shrieks, but her uncle, perfectly deaf to them, continued the flogging. When the third nine, given lengthwise, had been completed, Sir Edward put down the birch he had used and took a second from Maud. During the pause, his niece, with sobs and tears, earnestly implored him to let her off. For all reply, he again took up his station at her left side, and saying: "No, miss; I shall certainly not unstrap you; you have been far too naughty. I will punish you, and your lovely legs and bottom, to the fullest extent of the sentence, and teach you to be good, you bold hussey,

and give you a lesson you will not forget in a hurry"—
gave her nine more sound cuts; but this time, instead
of their being administered on the upper part of her
bottom, perpendicularly, they were given almost
horizontally on its lower part, where it joins the thigh.
Fresh yells and shrieks, all of no avail, were uttered by
the unhappy girl, who in her agony lifted up her head,
her shoulders being fastened down with the strap, and
prayed her uncle, by heaven, to spare her. But the
relentless rod still continued to cut into her tender and
now bleeding flesh, as she was told "she would receive
no mercy."

Maud's even voice continued to number the strokes,
and Maud herself seemed aflame, and the sight of the
agony her uncle was inflicting seemed to excite her
sensuality in an extraordinary degree. Her lips were
moist; her eyes swam; the eyelids drooped; and all the
indications of a very lovesick girl appeared in her. The
bleeding bottom, the tightly-strapped limbs, the
piercing cries, and the relentlessly inflicted punishment excited her strongest passions. She could have
torn Alice limb from limb; and she encouraged her
uncle, by rolling his balls and pulling and squeezing
his prick, to continue the punishment in the severest
manner.

She gloated over the numbers as she called them
out.

Sir Edward, too, seemed beside himself. His eyes
were as two flames; he watched every motion of Alice's
body; gloated upon all she displayed; could have made
his teeth meet in her delicate flesh, which he lacerated
with the rod yet more severely as his organ, already
excited to an enormous size, was still further enlarged
by Maud's hand.

At length, Alice's lower bottom having been well
wealed from right to left, as well as from left to right,

there remained but the nine strokes to be given lengthwise.

For these Sir Edward took the third birch from Maud, who by this time was standing with her legs wide apart, uttering little sounds and breathing little sighs of almost uncontrollable desire.

The unhappy culprit's yells had somewhat lessened, for the flowing blood had relieved the pain; and it had also been so severe that her sensitiveness to it had much diminished. But now, feeling the rod curling round her cunt, which, being all open and wet, was more than ever exposed, she yelled in a perfectly delirious manner.

After some few of these strokes had been given, her uncle asking her whether he was a wretch and a monster, as she had called him last night, she replied with vehement denials:—

"No! oh, no! oh! oh! oh! oh, no! Not a monster! Not a wretch! My own dear uncle, whom I love! Oh! oh! oh! My bottom burns! Oh! oh! It is on fire!"

"Will you be a good, obedient girl miss?"

"Yes! Yes! Yes! Oh! indeed—"

"And thank me for whipping you?"

"Yes; indeed I do."

"Whip well in, uncle," said Maud quietly, in her rich voice.

And he did so. Alice shrieked; flooded the floor with urine, and fainted!

Maud, beside herself, threw herself backwards on the long and broad divan—her breast, her legs (without drawers) wide extended. Sir Edward, throwing down the birch, threw himself upon her with fury. He inserted his enormous affair into her burning cunt, and he fucked her so violently that she almost fainted from delight.

When Alice came round, Sir Edward rose from

Maud's breast, and then Maud said, in clear tones:—

"Uncle, I told Alice yesterday evening, when she kept me so long before I could succeed in tying her hands, that I would take care it secured her an extra half-dozen."

"Oh, uncle! I beg Maud's pardon. Oh! after all I have gone through, let me off that half-dozen. Oh, dear Maud! do ask uncle to let me off. Oh, do! If I am birched any more I shall go mad! I shall—I shall indeed!"

Maud, still lying backwards on the couch, supported by a big, square pillow, said nothing. Her hands were clasped behind her head.

But Sir Edward said: "No miss; you can never be let off! You must have the half-dozen. It will be a lesson to you." And taking up the birch, he gave her six severe strokes, distributed evenly all over her bottom.

As they were being administered, Maud's left hand stole down to her waist and found its way between her legs.

While Alice was smothering her sobs and cries after her last half-dozen. Sir Edward again threw himself upon Maud and enjoyed her.

About ten minutes or a quarter of an hour later he proceeded to unstrap Alice.

She could not stand without Maud's help. The cushion and carpet were soaked with her urine and stained with her blood.

"You will to-morrow have a dozen on the trapeze, miss, for disgracing yourself in this beastly manner; you will write out fifty times, 'I pea'd like a mare before my uncle'; and for the next fortnight you will only pea twice in the twenty-four hours. And now come and kiss the rod and say: 'Thank you, my dear uncle, for the flogging you have given me.'"

Quite docilely she knelt down before him, kissed the

rod he held to her lips, and repeated the words.

"Will you be a good, obedient girl in future?"

"Yes, dear uncle; indeed I will!"

"Tha's a good thing. There is, you see, nothing like a good, sound flogging for a girl. Were the rod more in use how very much better women we should have. Now go with Maud and get some refreshment. I have various engagements, and shall not be in till dinner. After lunch you had better have a sleep." And so saying, he packed the two girls off to Alice's room, shut the yellow room door, and ringing for a footman, gave orders that the estate steward and horses should be in attendance at the front door in half an hour.

Maud and Alice went to the latter's room. By Maud's advice, Alice, who was so sore that she could scarcely move, got into bed and had some strong broth and Burgundy, and presently fell asleep. Maud spent her afternoon at an open window reclining in a lounge chair, pretending to read a novel, but in reality revelling in the reminiscences of the morning and meditating upon its delights—and wondering when she would get whipped next herself—until she was disturbed by some afternoon visitors.

CHAPTER III

MYSTERY

"My passions, however, are very strong;
but my Soul and Body are hostile sisters, and
the unhappy pair, like every imaginable
couple, lawful or unlawful, live in a perpetual
state of war."

—Mademoiselle de Maupin

Alice's slumbers were profound. For four or five hours she continued in the deepest sleep; but as consciousness gradually returned to her she dreamt: and dreamt, as she had never done before, of love. Her innocence was gone; and she would awake an experienced girl. Her dreams were of the softest pleasures; they were prompted by that new and wonderful sensation, under the influence of which she still was, which had been roused once for all while she lay ignominiously extended under her uncle's eye and received the cruel lashes of the birch upon the most secret and divine organ of her exquisite body. They, it is true, profaned the Temple; but they summoned to life the Divinity there enshrined. Her sexual instincts were aroused; she became conscious of her femininity. She felt the influence of Man; and a longing and insatiable desire to possess him. She now knew why she was beautiful, and in her dreams she pictured herself with soft delight—her velvety skin; her soft, plump, round arms; her throbbing bosom, and the ravishing sinuosities of her back—as being embraced by her uncle; she felt his weight on the front of her thighs; she imagined his tongue again between her lips. Her body glowed; her charms ripened; her mind, casting away the prudish veils with which it had so long been encumbered, already contemplated life in another and rosier light, and prepared her to bloom into that lovely and beautiful woman she was so soon to become.

Innocence! (so called) and virginity! in you we do not believe. Flowers, not of virtue, but of a dunghill; the conceptions and impure fruit of Shame, begotten upon Superstition—this is the pedigree we give to you. Ye are fostered by those who fatten upon the fears of the ignorant and weak-minded. Poor human creature, trembling upon the threshold of nature's holiest of holies; terror-stricken at the revelation of her most tremendous mystery about to be made you; you are swooped upon by the priest and called upon to deny your own nature! Your young and budding desires are described to you as sin, such as will condemn you hereafter to endless flame! Impurity is imputed to passion the most natural and the chastest which can possess the soul! and, outraged by the obscene imputation, it recoils in horror upon itself; but if initiated, if forearmed with knowledge, it crushes and stamps the foul tempter under foot, exclaiming: "Monster! the obscenity is in thee. Avaunt!"

Yes; we would have it enacted that all young creatures who had not by one and twenty years of age become women should be made so by compulsory union with a lover; and as the measure could not have a retrospective effect, all old maids—incomplete human creatures, mentally and physically, that they are—should be given three months and the services gratuitously of the most energetic advertising agency in the matrimonial market, and if they did not within that period form some true union and become the fulfilment and completement of some man (for no man is perfect until he includes woman), and, moreover, produce to the court incontestable proofs of the destruction of their maidenhead, that they should perish ignominiously as unnatural deformities. And so infatuated are many of these old deformities that we believe some would perish, although no doubt most would prefer forcible violation; and therefore those who, at the end of the three months, failed to produce the required evidence in court should be given one more chance. They should be placed in charge of a robust curate or other officer of the court, and this charge should be called marriage; the union to endure during the joint lives of the parties; and if at the end of the year the husband swore that all his efforts to storm his old virgin's citadel had failed, the marriage should be declared null; the old woman transfixed by the usher with a weapon to be duly provided for the purpose, and fitted to carry it out, and then strangled; and the curate or other officer provided forthwith with another beauty.

You will say this marriage of yours is a punishment; and we reply, perhaps marriage always is, but in this case that it ought to be so, as the men concerned—all of them—should be those, and those only, who have been indicted and convicted before a court composed of young women, of not having found and enjoyed a mistress before the completion of their twenty-fifth year. We apprehend that the class would not be very numerous, and "marriage" would therefore receive a salutary limitation.

But listen! Alice is rubbing her eyes and puzzling herself with reasons why she should be so possessed by the idea of, and longing for, her uncle, who had used her so cruelly. His being somehow or other overshadowed her, and she seemed to long to be absorbed in it. The strictest analysis of her craving only reduced it as far as a wish that he should take her in his arms and do with her what he wished—what that would be she knew not, but instinctively felt it would be something tremendous, which would entirely alter her whole subjective existence. He had seen her naked; he had reduced her, naked, to absolute submission to his will; he had inflicted upon her the cruellest pain; and the direct medium of the infliction of this pain had been the most secret portion of her body. Yet she delighted in the notion that he had seen her (with the exception solely of her stockings) completely nude; she enjoyed the idea that his hand had inflicted the stripes of which she still felt the effects; her breath came more quickly and she trembled with joy when she called to mind that it was to him she had been compelled to display, with the greatest possible humiliation to her, the most intimate recesses of her person and her most jealously-concealed charms without any reserve whatsoever.

She was much puzzled, and her perplexity was accentuated as she moved and felt how tender and how sore her bottom still was.

"Shall I ever be able to sit down again?" she wondered.

Then she recollected the catastrophe that had taken place the moment before she had swooned in that inexplicable ecstasy, and her cheeks flushed and grew hot with shame. And they flushed again and grew still hotter the second time when she recollected that she had to write out fifty times, "I pea'd like a mare before my uncle."

What a little beast she was, and how well she deserved flogging! How just and proper it was that for the next fortnight she should be allowed to relieve herself but twice in the twentyfour hours. The inconvenience would be a very proper lesson for so naughty a girl as she was.

In the midst of these reflections, in came Maud with some egg-flip.

"I would not let them disturb you for luncheon, dear, as I am sure uncle would wish you to be fresh in the evening; and, besides, you must have needed the rest dreadfully. How did you like your whipping?"

"Oh, Maud, it was dreadful! How cruelly severe uncle is."

"I suppose it has made you hate him?"

"No; that is the strangest thing about it. Last night I thought my hatred of him could not be sufficiently intense; but I now feel that I am completely mastered by him, and find that I am glad that it is so!"

"Dear Alice, that was my own experience."

"Has he whipped you, Maud?"

"Yes, dear; and sometimes I purposely do something in order to get myself flogged."

"How curious! When did he whip you first?"

"Oh, long ago. I must give you a full account of it another time. Did you faint with pain?"

"No. I seemed in heaven."

"You do not seem very much exhausted; but you had better eat this cake and egg-flip—it is better for you than tea—and let me look at that poor bottom and see what can be done for it."

So Maud sat down upon the bed, and Alice, to her own astonishment, now nothing loth, laid on her face while Maud removed all the bedclothes from her waist downwards, and, as they chatted, gently anointed her bottom with Vinolia cream, and gave her many a pleasant sensation by the adroit use she made of her hands and fingers.

Alice explained that she now felt a much more experienced girl, and much surprised at a former coyness, which she thought must have appeared extremely ridiculous.

She wondered that anyone could be prudish.

"Yes," said Maud, "It is want of education"— smiling—"and as for modesty, I verily believe innocent girls are only just one little bit less nasty than the very

British old maid herself," ended Maud, with a delicious laugh.

"And you, Alice," she went on, "how absurd you were when first you came, blushing at every second word, buttoning your dress up to your throat, wearing it on the ground, and almost screaming at the mere mention of an ankle."

"Oh, Maud, you do not know what I went through in the yellow room. When uncle turned up my petticoats and whipped me, and made me take off my own drawers before him—oh! oh! oh! the mere thought of it is fearful—and then when he put me across his knee and put his finger and thumb—"

"Where?" asked Maud.

"Oh, one in front and the other behind"—hiding her face with her hands.

"Like that?" said Maud.

"Yes. Just like that. Oh, Maud! oh, how nice! Well, dear, the wonder is that I am alive."

"The sweetest has to come yet, Alice dear. You said you were glad that uncle had mastered you. Do you not long for him?"

"Oh, Maud, I cannot tell you how I do. In such a strange way. I feel I could devour him!"

"Well, dear, all in good time. At any rate, you will not wish to conceal your charms now."

"Oh, no. I take quite a healthy delight in displaying them. I think a long dress quite immodest, because it must be a sign of a mind itching with nasty thoughts."

"Unless, indeed," she continued, after a moment's thoughtfulness, "it is because the natural growth has been checked."

"Oh, Alice, I am so glad that you are such a sensible girl. What splendid times we shall have together. I was never before so fully convinced how right uncle is in his opinion that there is nothing like a sound flogging for a girl. But although we have such a good opinion of ourselves, there are heaps of people who would condemn us with faint praise, and say we were only engagingly immoral. Uncle told me once it was because we were free and emancipated and capable of freely enjoying pleasure which the silly geese—although it is such a natural pleasure—think they are bound to deny themselves. There, Alice dear," ceasing her rubbing, which she had so caressingly done; "is the poor bottom better?"

"Yes, thank you, Maud dear, ever so much. I feel so surprised at being able to lie so unconcernedly before you."

"You see, Alice, you are emancipated—almost. Now you had better have a warm bath, and mind that you use the soap scented with attar of roses. Make a good lather, and bathe yourself all over with it. And then, my dear, you are to put on a low chemise of black silk trimmed with yellow, a yellow corset, black silk petticoats, yellow stockings and shoes, and a net dress with great big yellow spots all over it. It won't come below your knees, dear," said Maud, significantly, at which Alice gave a joyous laugh. "In your bosom you are to place some yellow roses which the gardener has been ordered to bring in on purpose for you."

"And," went on Maud, interrupting Alice, "you are to have your hair twisted up in one great coil and fastened with this arrow, which, you see, is studded with cairn gorms; and round your throat," opening a casket on the dressing table, "you are to put this necklace" (a magnificent one of cairn gorms set in brilliants). "By the bye, you are to tie your stockings with black, not yellow garters, and mind that the first petticoat you put on is that which is lined with yellow silk. Now mind, Alice, and do not make a mistake."

"Oh! how lovely!" cried Alice. "How good you are to

me you dear Maud, to take such an interest in me. I shall be dressed all in black and yellow. Why? I wonder."

"Because," mockingly answered Maud, "black and yellow are the devil's colours, and you have his beauty."

"Now, Maud, you are laughing at me. I wonder what you will wear?"

"Oh, something not so striking, dear. You see, it is your turn to-night. You are to be the heroine of to-night. And before I go to dress, I must say goodbye to you, Alice, for I shall not have another opportunity of doing so during the evening, and to-morrow I shall not see you girl again."

"What on earth do you mean, Maud?" asked Alice, experiencing an unaccountable sensation of which she did not understand the significance. "You are not going away, surely?" in alarm.

"Oh, no, you dear goose," replied Maud. "I only meant that I should not see you a girl to-morrow because in all probability you will then be a woman," and the room rang with the musical and merry peal of laughter Maud gave.

"You speak in riddles, dear. I wish you would explain, and not tease me so."

"Not I," said Maud. "Write to Miss Ada Ballin, of the *Ladies' Pictorial*, duly enclosing a coupon, and she will tell you the difference between a girl and a woman; or, by the bye, as it is not the sort of matter the editor (who ought to be circumcised) would allow an explanation of publicly, you had better send her a fee for a private reply; or, better still," she went on maliciously, "ask her for the address of a medical man competent to set forth the mystery personally to you, and," said Maud, in shrieks of laughter at her own wit, "Miss Ada Ballin will certainly send it, if you enclose a stamped, addressed envelope so that it may be sent you privately, as it would be a violation of professional etiquette to publish it; and misses are said to hate violation of every sort. Come! Come! Alice," seeing that Alice began to pout, thinking that Maud was laughing at her, "do not be offended at my nonsense. You will know all about it by to-morrow yourself. Dear me, there's the dressing bell. Only an hour to dinner. Whoever would have thought it was so late?"

"Why not stop and dress here?"

"No; not to-night, dear. One word more, Alice. I heard that you are, for the next fortnight, only to go somewhere twice every day. Now, dear, take my advice and do it late as you can after dinner, and in the morning after you have left the yellow room, if you have to go there. And I know you have to to-morrow."

"Yes; I have; but I do not dread it so much. But I am not going to be birched; am I?"

"No, dear. You are going to have a dozen on the trapeze, which is in some respects worse. I can't stop to explain, though, because, if I do, I shall be late, and then I should be birched."

"Oh, Maud! Very well, dear, I will take your advice, with thanks."

"I am sure you will find it good. Here's Janet. I must run off."

"What? Miss Maud in here after the bell has rung. Get off to your room, miss, or ye'll have the tawse, and nae doot aboot it."

Then the old Scotch maid, without ado, stripped Alice stark naked and conducted her to her bath. Though she treated her like an infant, and gave her a pinch and a smack or two on the buttocks if she considered Alice was slow in obeying her directions, yet she washed and dressed her with tenderness and care, mingled with a certain amount of reverence for the girl's absolute loveliness.

"She's a bonnie bit lassie anyhow; but, gudeness guide us, what a lashing she has had about her puir body."

She would not, however, allow any nonsense on Alice's part. The yellow corset was laced as she thought proper. Alice's protests were unheeded, and her breasts were placed in what she still considered unnecessary prominence. The roses were placed between them. The magnificent hair, done up in one great coil, was rolled up on the top of her shapely little head and fixed with the arrow, which sparkled with the brilliants in the setting of the great cairn gorms. At last her toilette was complete, and, bewilderingly and bewitchingly beautiful, exciting not only her rugged Scotch attendant's admiration (who exclaimed: "It was not work thrown away to deck so bonnie a bairn as hersell"), but her own, she descended to the drawing-room with that gently undulating motion which adds so greatly to the fascinations even of those who may otherwise possess charms of the highest degree.

In the drawing-room she found Maud and Sir Edward; to her surprise, there was no one else. But Sir Edward was dressed "fin de siècle," and was gay with a yellow rose in his buttonhole. And Alice blushed with gratification when she noticed, as she did the instant she saw it was precisely the same kind of rose as those in her bosom and the single one in her hair. Maud looked demurely lovely, and, though dressed in the height of fashion, had somehow good-naturedly managed to efface herself so that she might not interfere with Alice's triumph.

Then they went to dinner, Alice, again to her surprise, on her uncle's arm and at the head of the table.

"Maud has abdicated in your favour to-night, my

dear, although, it is true, it is not your week. But she has only surrendered the glories to you, so do not be disturbed about the responsibilities," her uncle added, kindly, noticing a slightly anxious expression appear.

The table groaned with summer fruits in chased gold dishes, and was decorated entirely with white roses. Never did soup taste more delicious or were its odours and flavours more appreciated; never did the chicken of the ocean, the twisted whiting, or the lordly salmon or the saintly sole meet, or were better qualified to meet, with heartier approval; never was the wine in better order—although Alice thought the Chablis (La Moutonne) a little too heavy. The champagne, iced to a nicety by the portly butler, was not on this occasion Dry Monopole, but a sweeter wine, which pleased Alice more. It soon added cordiality to a gay and merry scene. Sir Edward sent his compliments to the delighted *chef* upon the production by him of a work of art which had occupied that artist ever since he had received the necessary hint from Maud. It reminded her, said Alice, "of nothing so much as of a wedding cake," at which Maud covertly smiled. It was a representation in confectionery of Venus, her cupids, her doves, and her triumphs. The figure reminded Alice for a moment of her own. It was not until afterwards she discovered that in a panel of her bedroom was fixed a secret camera, and that while the night before she had stood for but a minute naked before her glass, Sir Edward had found time to take an instantaneous photograph of her, and that it was this photograph which, shown to the enraptured *chef* by Maud, had proved his inspiration. Sir Edward was enraptured, too, as he gazed, and the message for his cook was delivered with such warmth to his own valet that that functionary, immoveable although he appeared, was quite startled in reality. And his description or his master's earnestness pleased the genius of the kitchen quite as much as the jewel which Sir Edward had taken off his own finger and sent with the message. Monsieur Philippe felt that the ambition of a lifetime was to some extent attained, and thanked his gods that he possessed a master who could appreciate the efforts of genius.

After dinner was served that rare growth of Burgundy "Romance Conti," than which no Clos Vougeot or Chambertin or any other growth of the Côte d'Or is more delicious. Château-Laffite, Château-La-Rose, Château-Margaux suggest, they do not equal it. And they are clarets. It is a wine which fills the veins with an elixir of life, and so Alice thought it. Why she was made so much of; why she was so petted, she could not understand. Was that courteous and gallant cavalier opposite her at the other end of the table, more like a lover in his addresses than her guardian, the same cruel and relentless uncle who had flogged her with such merciless severity in the morning, and who was, she recollected with wonder, again to punish her on the morrow? And then she called to mind herself. Was the laughing girl, full of joke and mirth; the beauty decked out in black and yellow, displaying with such artless coquetry her many charms, and giving herself in her high spirits so many winning airs, and feeling so much at ease, although she had no drawers on, as Maud and her uncle knew, and although her dress only barely came down to her knees, at all of which she was now rather more pleased than otherwise—the same Alice she had formerly known, dressed in a high-fitting, tight, dowdy brown garment, and expiring with shame at the sight of half an inch of leg? She laughed with joy to feel that she was becoming free from such ridiculous notions, and rejoiced at the growing sense of liberty to enjoy the possession of her charms, and to employ the power they gave her to the uttermost.

After dinner they went to a room upstairs, panelled with rose-coloured silk and hung with water-colours.

CHAPTER IV

MYSTERY UNVEILED

"Away!" she cried, "grave face and solemn sighs;
Kiss and be merry! Preach the sermon after.
Give me the careless dance and sparkling eyes;
Let me be wooed with kisses, songs, and laughter!"
—The Monks of Thelema.

Then up he got and donned his clothes,
And dupped the chamber door;
Let in the maid that out a maid
Never departed more.
—Old Song: Shakespeare.

It was a beautiful summer's night. The air was heavily laden with the sweet perfume of the flowers in the garden below the windows, which were thrown wide open. There were besides several china vases, or rather bowls, standing about the room, full of roses, of shades varying from the deepest crimson to the softest blush scarcely more than suggested upon the delicate petal. The only sounds were the gentle rustle of the summer zephyr amongst the trees and the weird hoot of the owls. The deeply-shaded lamps gave animation to the rosy tints of the boudoir. They were emphasized by the yellow flame of the fire which, notwithstanding the season, crackled merrily in the grate. (A fire upon a summer's night is an agreeable thing.) Between it and Alice there at once appeared to be something in common. She and the fire were the only two black and gold things in the rosy apartment. The fierce flame struck Alice as being a very adequate expression of the love she felt seething in her veins. She felt intoxicated with passion and desire, and capable of the most immoral deeds, the more shocking the better.

This naughty lust was soon to have at least some gratification. Maud had seated herself at the piano—

an exquisite instrument in a Louis Seize case—and had played softly some snatches of Schubert's airs, and Alice had been reclining some minutes on a rose-coloured couch—a beautiful spot of black and yellow, kept in countenance by the fire—showing two long yellow legs, when Sir Edward noticed that every time she altered her position she endeavoured, with a slightly tinged cheek, to pull her frock down. Of course he had been gazing at the shapely limbs and trying to avail himself of every motion, which could not fail to disclose more—the frock being very short—to see above her knee. He thought once that he had succeeded in catching a glimpse of the pink flesh above the yellow stocking.

Alice, sensible of her uncle's steadfast observation, was more and more overwhelmed with the most bewitching confusion; her coy and timid glances, her fruitless efforts to hide herself, only serving to make her the more attractive.

Maud looked on with amusement from the music-stool, where she sat pouring liquid melody from her pretty fingers, and mutely wondering whatever had come over Alice, and whatever had become of the healthy delight in displaying her charms of which she had boasted before dinner. Maud felt very curious to know how it would end.

"Alice," at length said her uncle, with a movement of impatience, "have you begun to write out that sentence I told you to write out fifty times?"

"Oh, no, uncle! I have not."

"Well, my dear, you had better set to work. It will suggest wholesome reflections."

So Alice got up and got some ruled paper, an inkstand, and a quill pen; then, seating herself at a Chippendale table, began to fiddle with the pen and ink.

Her uncle continued to watch her intently. Maud had ceased to play, and had thrown herself carelessly on the couch which Alice had just left. Maud's dress, too, was quite low and very short; but in the most artless way she flung herself backwards upon the sofa and clasped her hands behind her head, thus showing her arms, neck, bust, and breast to the fullest advantage; and pulling her left foot up to her thigh, made a rest with the left knee for the right leg, which she placed across it, thus fully displaying her legs in their open-work stockings and her thighs encased in loose flesh-coloured silk drawers tied with crimson ribbons. Her attitude and abandon were not lost upon Sir Edward.

Alice's sensations were dreadful. How could she, there, under her uncle's eye, write that she had "pea'd"? And not only "pea'd", but with shame and anger she recollected the sentence ran, "like a mare!"— like an animal; like a beast; as she had seen them in the street. And all "before her uncle." Whatever would become of her if she had to write this terrible sentence; to put so awful a confession into her own handwriting; to confide such a secret fifty times over with her own hand to paper? If it was ever found out she would be ruined—her reputation would be gone—no one would have anything to say to her—she would have to fly to the mountains and the caves. She had not realized until it came to actually writing it out how difficult, how terrible, how impossible it was for her to do it. If her uncle knew, surely he would not insist. He could not wish her to humiliate herself to such an extent; to ruin and destroy herself with her own handwriting; neither could he have realized what it would be for her to write such a thing. While these thoughts were passing through her mind, she kept unconsciously pulling and dragging at her frock. If only she could cover herself up. So much of her legs showed; and the long yellow stockings made them so conspicuous under her black frock. Although they were above her knee, unless she kept her legs close together she could not help showing her black garters. And her arms and her neck and her breast were all bare. She began to feel almost sulky.

"Well, Alice," at length said her uncle; "when are you going to begin?"

"Oh, uncle! it is dreadful to have to say such a thing in my own handwriting—I am sure you have never thought how dreadful."

"You must chronicle in your own handwriting what you did, miss. Writing what you did is not so bad as doing it. And you will not only write it, but you shall sign it with your name, so that everyone may know what a naughty girl you were."

"Oh, uncle! oh, uncle! I can't. You will burn it when it is done; won't you?"

"No; certainly not. It shall be kept as a proof of how naughty you can be."

And as she kept tugging at her frock and not writing, her uncle said:—

"Maud, will you fetch the dress-suspender? It will keep her dress out of her way."

Maud discharged her errand with alacrity. In less than three minutes she had returned with a band of black silk, from which hung four long, black silk ribbons. Making Alice stand up, Maud slipped her arms under her petticoats and put the band round Alice's waist next her skin, buckling it behind, and edged it up as high as the corset, which Janet had not left loose, would allow. The four ribbons hung down far below the frock, two at the right and two at the left hip—one ribbon in front, the other at the back.

Maud then walked Alice over into the full blaze of

the fire. Putting her arms round her and bending down, she took the ribbons at Alice's left side one in each hand, and then pulled them up and joined them on Alice's right shoulder in a bow. The effect, of course, was to bundle half Alice's petticoats and dress up about her waist, disclosing her left leg from the end of the stocking naked. Maud, with little ceremony, then turned her round, and, taking the ribbons at her right side, tied them across her left shoulder, thus removing the other half of Alice's covering and displaying the right leg. She then carefully arranged the frock and petticoats, smoothing them out, tightening the ribbons, and settling the bows. And by the time she had finished, from the black band round her waist nearly to her garters, Alice was in front and behind perfectly naked—her breast and arms and thighs and navel and buttocks. The lower petticoat was, it will be remembered, lined with yellow, and the inside was turned out. It and the stockings and the two black bands intensified her nakedness. She would sooner have been, she felt, stripped entirely of every shred of clothing than have had on those garments huddled about her waist, and those stockings, which, she instinctively knew, only heightened the exhibition of her form and directed the gaze to all she most wished to conceal.

"Now, miss," said her uncle, "this will save you the trouble of vain and silly efforts to conceal yourself."

"Oh, uncle! uncle! how can you disgrace me so?"

"Disgrace you, my dear? What nonsense! You are not deformed. You are perfectly exquisite. With," he continued, passing his hand over her, "a skin like satin."

Feeling his hand, Alice experienced a delicious thrill, which her uncle noticing, recommended her to sit down and write out her imposition—a task which was now a hundred times more difficult. However could she, seated in a garb which only displayed her nakedness in the most glaring manner, write such words?

"Alice," said he, "you are again becoming refractory."

Putting his arm round her, he sat down and put her face downwards across his left knee. "You must have your bottom smacked. That will bring you to your senses." (Smack—smack—smack—smack—smack—smack.)

"Oh, uncle! don't! Oh!"—struggling—"I will write anything!"—smack—"oh! how you sting!"—smack—smack—"oh! oh! oh! Your hand is so hard."

Then, slipping his hand between her legs, he tickled her clitoris until she cooed and declared she would take a delight in saying and writing and doing the "most shocking things."

"Very well, miss! Then go and write out what I told you; sign it; and bring it to me when it is finished."

So Alice seated herself—the straw seat of the chair pricking her bottom—resolved, however, to brazen out her nakedness, and wrote with a trembling hand: "I pea'd like a mare before my uncle; I pea'd like a mare before my uncle; I pea'd like a mare before my uncle." Before she had half completed her task, she was so excited and to such an extent under the influence of sensual and voluptuous feelings that she could not remain still; and she felt the delicate hair in front about her cunt grow moist. Before she had completed the fiftieth line she was almost beside herself.

At last, for the fiftieth time, she wrote:—

"I pea'd like a mare before my uncle."

And with a shudder, signed it, "Alice Darvell."

During her task Maud had looked at what she was writing over her shoulder, and Alice glowed with shame. So had her uncle; but Alice was surprised to find she rather liked his seeing her disgrace, and felt inclined to nestle close up to him.

Now Maud had gone to bed, and she was to take her task to her uncle.

He was seated in a great chair near the fire, looking very wide awake indeed. He might have been expected to have been dozing. But there was too lovely a girl in the room for that. He looked wide awake indeed, and there was a fierce sparkle in his eye as his beautiful ward, in her long yellow stockings and low dress, her petticoats turned up to her shoulders, and blushing deeply, approached him with her accomplished penance.

She handed it to him.

"So you did, Alice," said he, "so you did," sitting bolt upright, "pea like a mare before me, and here is, I see," turning over a page or two, "your own signature to the confession."

"Oh, uncle, it is true; but do not let anyone know. I know I disgraced myself and behaved like a beast; but I am so sorry."

"But you deserved your punishment."

"Yes; I know I did. Only too well."

He drew her down upon his knee, and placed his right arm round her waist, while he tickled her legs and her groin and her abdomen, and lastly her clitoris, with his hand and fingers.

He let her, when she was almost overcome by the violence of her sensations, slip down between his knees, and as she was seeking how most effectually to caress him, he directed her hands to his penis and his testicles. In a moment of frenzy she tore open his trousers, lifted his shirt, and saw the excited organ, the goal and Ultima Thule of feminine delight. He pressed down her head, and, despite the resistance she at first made, the inflamed and distended virility was very quickly placed between the burning lips of her mouth. Its taste and the transport she was in induced her to suck it violently. On her knees before her uncle, tickling, sucking, licking his penis, then looking in his face and recommencing, the sweet girl's hands again very quickly found their way to his balls.

At last, excited beyond his self-control, gazing through his half-closed lids at the splendid form of his niece at his feet—her bare back and shoulders—the breast which, sloping downwards from her position, he yet could see—her bare arms—the hands twiddling and manipulating and kneading with affection and appreciation his balls; his legs far apart, himself thrown back gasping in his arm chair; his own most sensitive and highly excited organ in the dear girl's hot mouth, tickled with the tip of her dear tongue, and pinched with her dear, pretty, cruel ivory teeth—Sir Edward could contain himself no longer and, grasping Alice's head with both his hands, he pushed his weapon well into her mouth and spent down her throat. He lay back in a swoon of delight, and the girl, as wet as she could be, leant her head against his knee, almost choked by the violence of the delightful emission, and stunned by the mystery revealed to her. How she loved him! How she dandled that sweet fellow! How she fondled him! What surreptitious licks she gave him! She could have eaten her uncle.

In about twenty minutes he had recovered sufficiently to speak, and she sat with her head resting against the inside of his right leg, looking up into his face; her own legs stretched out underneath his left one—she was sitting on the floor.

"Alice, you bold, bad girl, to pea like a mare. I hope you feel punished now."

"Oh no, uncle, it was delightful. Does it give you

pleasure? I will suck you again," taking his penis, to his great excitement, again in her warm little palm, "if you wish."

"My dear, do you want to pea?"

"Yes; before I go to bed."

"Then here is the key. Run along and go to bed."

"Oh, I would rather stay with you."

"Although I have whipped you and birched you and smacked you and made you disgrace yourself?"

"Yes, dear uncle. It has done me good. Don't send me away."

"Go, Alice, to bed. I will come to you there."

"Oh, you dear uncle, how nice. Oh, do let down my things for me before I go. Some of the servants may see me."

"And," she continued, after an instant's pause, with a blush, and looking down, "I want to be for you alone."

Touched by her devotion, her uncle loosed the ribbons; let fall, as far as they would, her frock and petticoats; and giving her a kiss, and not forgetting to use his hand under her clothes in a manner which caused her again to cry out with delight, allowed her to trip off to her bedroom. But not without the remark that she had induced him to do that which did not add to her appearance; for the rich, full, and well-developed girlish form had been simply resplendent with loveliness in the garments huddled about her waist; the petticoat lining of yellow silk relieved by the black bands from her waist to her shoulder crossing each other, and bits of her black frock, with its large yellow spots, appearing here and there. And as the eye travelled downwards from the pink flesh of the swelling breasts to the smooth pink thighs, it noted with rapture that the clothes concealed only what needed not concealment, and revealed with the greatest effect what did; and, still descending, dwelt entranced upon the well-turned limbs, whose outlines and curves the tight stockings so clearly defined. Sir Edward, who had made her stand facing him, and also with her back to him, was much puzzled, although so warm a devotee of the Venus Callipyge, whether he preferred the back view of her lovely legs, thighs, bottom, back, nuque, and queenly little head, with its suggestion of fierce and cruel delight; or the front, showing the mount and grotto of Venus, the tender breasts, the dimpled chin and sparkling eyes, with the imaginations of soft pleasures and melting trances which the sloping and divided thighs suggested and invited.

The first thing which Alice noticed upon reaching her room was the little supper-table laid for two; and the next that there were black silk sheets on her bed. The sight of the supper—the chocolate, the tempting cakes and biscuits, the rich wines in gold mounted jugs, the Nuremburg glasses, the bonbons, the crystallized fruit, the delicate omelette—delighted her; but the black sheets had a somewhat funereal and depressing effect.

"What can Maud have been thinking of, my dear, to put black sheets on the bed; and to-night of all nights in the year?" asked Sir Edward, angrily, the instant he entered the apartment, and hastily returning to the sitting-room, he rang and ordered Janet up. She was directed to send Miss Maud to "my niece's room, and in a quarter of an hour to put *pink* silk sheets on the bed there."

Then Sir Edward returned, and giving Alice some sparkling white wine, which with sweet biscuits she said she would like better than anything else, he helped himself to a bumper of red—standing expecting Maud's appearance. Alice was seated in a cosy chair, toasting her toes.

Presently Maud arrived in a lovely déshabille, her rich dark hair tumbling about her shoulders, the dressing-gown not at all concealing the richly-embroidered robe de nuit beneath it, and the two garments clinging closely to her form, setting off her lovely svelte figure to perfection. Her little feet were encased in low scarlet slippers embroidered with gold, so low cut as to show the whole of the white instep.

Her manner was hurried and startled, but this pretty dismay increased her attractions.

"Maud," asked her uncle, "what do you mean by having had black sheets put on this bed, when I distinctly said they were to be pink?"

"Indeed, indeed, uncle, you said black."

"How dare you contradict me, miss, and so add to your offence? You have been of late very careless indeed. You shall be soundly punished. Go straight to the yellow room," he went on to the trembling girl. "I will follow you in a few moments and flog you in a way that you will recollect. Eighteen stripes with my riding-whip and a dozen with the cat-o'-nine-tails."

"Oh, uncle," she gasped.

"Go along, miss."

Alice, to her surprise, although she had some little feeling of distress for Maud, felt quite naughty at the idea of her punishment; and, noticing her uncle's excitement, concluded instinctively that he also felt similar sensations. She was, consequently, bold enough, without rising, to stretch out her hand and to press outside his clothes the gentleman underneath with whom she had already formed so intimate an acquaintance, asking as she did so whether he was going to be very severe.

"Yes," he replied, moving to and fro (notwithstanding which she kept her hand well pressed on him). "I shall lash her bottom until it bleeds and she yells for mercy."

"O, uncle!" said Alice, quivering with a strange thrill.

"Go to the room, Alice. I shall follow in a moment."

Poor Maud was in tears, and Alice, much affected at this sight, attempted to condole with her.

"The riding-whip is terribly severe; however I shall bear it I can't tell; and then that terrible cat afterwards; it will drive me mad."

"Oh, Maud, I am so sorry."

"And I made no mistake. He said black sheets. The fact is, your beauty has infuriated him, and he wants to tear me to pieces."

Sir Edward returned without trousers, wearing a kilt.

"Now come over here, you careless hussy," and indicating two rings in the floor quite three feet apart, he made her stretch her legs wide, so as to place her feet near the rings, to which Alice was made to strap them by the ankles. "I will cure you of your carelessness and inattention to orders. Your delicate flesh will feel this rod's cuts for days. Off with your dressing-gown; off with your night-dress." Alice was dazzled by her nakedness, the ripeness of her charms, the whiteness of her skin, the plump, soft, round bottom, across which Sir Edward laid a few playful cuts, making the girl call out, for, fixed as she was, she could not struggle.

Alice then, by her uncle's direction, placed before Maud a trestle, the top of which was stuffed and covered with leather, and which reached just to her middle. Across this she was made to lie, and two rings on the other side were drawn down and fixed her elbows, so that her head was almost on the floor, and her bottom, with its skin tight, well up in the air. Her legs, of course, were well apart. The cruelty of the attitude inflamed Alice.

"Give me the whip," said her uncle. As she handed the heavy weapon to him, he added, "stand close to me while I flog her, and," slipping his hand up her petticoats on to her inflamed and moist organ, "keep your hand upon me while I do so."

Alice gave a little spring as he touched her. Her own animal feelings told her what was required of her.

Maud was crying softly.

"Now, miss," as the whip cut through the air, "it is your turn"—swish—a great red weal across the bottom and a writhe of agony—"you careless"—swish—"wicked"—swish—"disobedient"—swish—"obstinate girl."

"Oh, uncle! oh! oh! oh! oh! I am sorry, oh, forgive—"—swish—"no, miss"—swish—"no forgiveness. Black sheets, indeed"—swish—swish—swish—"I will cure you, my beauty."

Maud did her best to stifle her groans, but it was clear that she was almost demented with the exquisite torture the whip caused her every time it cut with relentless vigour into her bleeding flesh. Sir Edward did not spare her. The rod fell each time with unmitigated energy.

"Spare the rod and spoil you, miss. Better spoil your bold, big bottom than that," he observed, as he pursued the punishment. The more cruel it became the greater Alice found grew her uncle's and her own excitement, until at last she scarcely knew how to contain herself. At the ninth stripe, Sir Edward crossed over to Maud's right to give the remaining nine the other way across.

Swish—swish—swish—fell the heavy whip, the victim's moans and prayers absolutely unheeded.

"A girl must have her bare bottom whipped"—

swish—"occasionally; there is nothing"—swish—"so excellent for her"—swish—"it teaches her to mind what is told her"—swish—"it knocks all false shame"—swish—"out of her; there is no mock modesty left about a young—lady after"—swish—"she has had her bottom under the lash."

Alice trembled when she saw the cat-o'-nine-tails, made of hard, tightly twisted whip-cords, each tail bearing several knots, and when she looked at the bleeding bottom she grew sick and pale. But when her uncle began to lecture Maud as he caressingly drew the terrible scourge through his fingers, and to tell her that for a hardened girl such as she was a whip was insufficient punishment, and that she must also be subjected to the cat's claws, Alice began to revive, and she noticed that, while Sir Edward again approached boiling point, Maud gave as much lascivious movement as her tight bonds permitted.

But the first three strokes, given from left to right, evoked piercing yells and shrieks; the next three, given across the other way, cries and howls of the wildest despair, followed by low sobs. The blood flowed freely and was spattered about the room. Alice felt some on her face and arms.

"You will not forget again, I know," said Sir Edward, as he wielded the terrible instrument. "You careless, naughty girl, how grateful you should be to me for taking the trouble to chastise you thus. The cat has quite irresistible arguments, has she not?"

The last six were given lengthwise, first along the legs, then round the bottom, and lastly on the cunt. Maud's roars and yells were redoubled; but in an ecstasy of delight she lost her senses at the last blow.

Alice, too, was mad with excitement. Rushing off, as directed, to her room, she, as her uncle had also bid her do, tore off all her clothing and dived into the pink sheets, rolling about with the passion the sight of the whipping had stimulated to an uncontrollable degree.

Sir Edward, having summoned Janet to attend Maud, hastened to follow Alice.

Divesting himself of all his clothing, he tore the bedclothes off the naked girl who lay on her back, inviting him to her arms, and to the embrace of which she was still ignorant, by the posture nature dictated to her, and looking against the pink sheet a perfect rose of loveliness. Sir Edward sprang upon her in a rush and surge of passion which bore him onwards with the irresistible force of a flowing sea. In a moment he, notwithstanding her cries, was between her already separated legs, clasping her to him, while he directed, with his one free hand, his inflamed and enormous penis to her virgin cunt. Already it had passed the lips and was forcing its way onwards, impelled, by the reiterated plunges of Sir Edward, before Alice could realize what was happening. At last she turns a little pale, and her eyes open wide and stare slightly in alarm, while, finding that her motion increases the assault and the slight stretching of her cunt, she remains still. But the next moment, remembering what had occurred when it was in her mouth, it struck her that the same throbbing and shooting and deliciously warm and wet emission might be repeated in the lower and more secret part of her body, and that if, as she hoped and prayed it might be, it was, she would expire of joy. These ideas caused a delightfull tremor and a few movements of the buttocks, which increased Sir Edward's pleasure and enabled him to make some progress. But at length the swelling of his organ and his march into the interior began to hurt, and she became almost anxious to withdraw from the amorous encounter. His arms, however, held her tight. She could not get him from between her legs, and she was being pierced in the tenderest portion of her body by a man's great thing, like a horse's. Oh, how naughty she felt! And yet how it hurt! How dreadful it was that he should be able to probe her with it and detect all her sensations by means of it, while on the other hand, she was made sensible there, and by means of it, of all he felt.

"Oh! uncle! Oh! dear, dear uncle! Oh! oh! oh! oh! Wait one minute! Oh! not so hard! Oh, dear, don't push any further—oh, it is so nice; but it hurts! Oh, do stop! don't press so hard! Oh! oh! oh! Oh! please don't! oh! it hurts! Oh! I shall die! You are tearing me open! you are indeed! Oh! oh! oh!"

"If you don't"—push—push—"hold me tight and push against me, Alice, I will—yes, that's better—flog your bottom until it bleeds and the blood runs down to your heels, you bold girl. No, you shan't get away. I will get right into you. Don't," said he, clawing her bottom with his hands and pinching its cheeks severely, "slip back. Push forward."

"Oh! I shall die! Oh! oh! oh!" as she felt she pinches, and jerked forward, enabling Sir Edward to make considerable advance, "Oh! I shall faint; I shall die! Oh, stop! Oh!" as she continued her involuntary motion upwards and downwards, "you hurt excruciatingly." He folded her more closely to him, and, altogether disregarding her loud cries, proceeded to divest her of her maidenhead, telling her that if she did not fight bravely he would punish her till she thought she was being flayed alive; that he would tear her bottom for her with hooks; and he slipped a hand down behind her, and got the middle finger well into her arse.

After this, victory was assured. A few more shrieks and spasms of mingled pleasure and pain, when Sir Edward, who had forced himself up to the hymen and had made two or three shrewed thrusts at it, evoking loud gasps and cries from his lovely ward, drew a long sigh, and with a final determined push sunk down on her bosom, while she, emitting one sharp cry, found her suffering changed into a transport of delight. She clasped her uncle with frenzy to her breast, and throbbed and shook in perfect unison with him, while giving little cries of rapture and panting—with half-closed lids, from under which rolled a diamond tear or two—for the breath of which her ecstasy had robbed her.

Several moments passed, the silence interrupted only by inarticulate sounds of gratification. Sir Edward's mouth was glued to hers, and his tongue found its way between its ruby lips and sought hers. Overcoming her coyness, the lovely girl allowed him to find it, and no sooner had they touched than an electric thrill shot through her; Sir Edward's penis, which had never been removed, again began to swell; he recommenced his (and she her) upward and downward movements and again the delightful crisis occurred—this time without the intense pain Alice had at first experienced, and with very much greater appreciation of the shock, which thrilled her from head to foot and seemed to penetrate and permeate the innermost recesses of her being.

Never had she experienced, or even in her fondest moments conceived, the possibility of such transports. She had longed for the possession of her uncle; she had longed to eat him, to become absorbed in him; and she now found the appetite gratified to the fullest extent, in a manner incredibly sweet. To feel his weight upon the front of her thighs—to feel him between her legs, her legs making each of his a captive; the most secret and sensitive and essentially masculine organ of his body inside that part of hers of which she could not think without a blush; and the mutual excitement, the knowledge and consciousness each had of the other's most intimate sensations, threw her into an ecstasy. How delicious it was to be a girl; how she enjoyed the contemplation of her charms; how supremely, overpoweringly delightful it was to have a lover in her embrace to appreciate and enjoy them! How delicious was love!

Sir Edward, gratified at length, rose and congratulated Alice upon her newborn womanhood; kissed her, and thanked her for the intense pleasure she had given him.

After some refreshment, as he bade her good-night, the love-sick girl once more twined her arms about him, while slipping her legs on to the edge of the bed, she lay across it and managed to get him between them; then, drawing him down to her bosom, cried, "Once more, dear uncle; once more before you go."

"You naughty girl," he answered, slightly excited; "well, I will if you ask me."

"Oh, please, do, uncle. Please do it again."

"Do what again?"

"Oh! It. You know. What—what—what," hiding her face sweetly, "you have done to me twice already."

"Don't you know what it is called?"

"No. I haven't the slightest idea.'

"It is called 'fucking.' Now, if you want it done again, you must ask to be fucked," said he, his instrument assuming giant proportions.

"Oh, dear, I do want it ever so; but however I can ask for it—please uncle—will—will you, please— please—f—f—fu—fuck me once more before you go?" and she lay back and extended her legs before him in the divinest fashion.

In a moment he was between them; his prick inserted; his lips again upon hers; and in a few moments more they were again simultaneously overcome by that ecstasy of supernatural exquisiteness of which unbridled passion has alone attempted to fathom the depths, and that without reaching them.

Exhausted mentally and physically by her experiences and the exercises of the evening, Alice, as she felt the lessening throbs of her uncle's engine, found she was losing herself and consciousness in drowsiness. Her uncle placed her in a comfortable posture upon the great pillow, and throwing the sheet over her, heard her murmured words of thanks and love as she fell asleep with a smile upon her face. Janet came and tucked her up comfortably. And she slept profoundly.

CHAPTER V

PUNISHMENT

Whipping grown girls is a pastime rare
Few males, if called on, could refuse to share.
—*Romance of Chastisement.*

Alice lay awake next morning listening to the birds, in a sweet trance as the recollection on which she dwelt of what she had passed through the night before. She felt completely changed, and could she have seen the dark stains upon the crimson sheet under her, she would have known that she really was so.

She met Maud in the breakfast-room and was warmly greeted by her.

"Well, love; well, Alice?" cried she, clasping both her hands in her own and gazing into her face with a glance in which there was deep meaning.

"Oh, Maud!" ejaculated Alice, blushing, and then, to turn the subject, "how are you, dear, after that terrible flogging? I could almost have cried at what you suffered at one moment, and yet I could have made uncle tear you in pieces the next."

"Yes," said Maud; "I have experienced the feeling. The result was that you and your uncle enjoyed yourselves the more. Now, wasn't it?"

After breakfast Alice remembered that she had to go straight to the yellow room. She did so without much dread, feeling that she could not have worse to go through than she had already suffered; although one or two chance expressions of Maud had made her doubtful of this conclusion; and the cold sternness of her uncle startled and alarmed her after his warmth and tenderness of the preceding evening. When he met her and wished her good morning in the breakfast-room he was apparently absolutely unconscious, and certainly totally forgetful, of what had passed.

Alice went with Maud arm-in-arm to the yellow room, wondering what the trapeze would be like.

Her uncle soon followed her and locked the door. He had a long carriage-whip and some sheets of paper which she recognised in his hand.

"You are Miss Alice Darvell, and this is your handwriting and signature?" asked he severely, showing the papers to her.

"Oh yes, uncle; they are," answered the girl, trembling with fright.

"You pea'd like a mare before your uncle, eh, miss?"

"I—I—I couldn't help it."

"Did you?"

"Y—ye—yes!"

"Well, you shall be flogged like a mare. Strip yourself."

"Oh, uncle!"

"Strip yourself absolutely naked, or," he said, raising the whip and lightly slashing it about her legs, for her frock only came down to her knees, "you shall have double."

She jumped as she felt the lash sting her calves, and drew up her legs one after another.

Then, seeing her uncle's arm again raised, she began to quickly undo her bodice and slip off her frock; her petticoats and corset soon followed, and, lastly, slipping off her chemise, she stood naked except for her long stockings, and covered with a most bewildering air of shame, not knowing whether to cover her face or not, or how to dispose of her hands and arms.

"Take off your shoes and stockings," said her uncle.

She had to do so seated in her nakedness, and the action added extremely to confusion.

Sir Edward then went to a bracket or flat piece of wood screwed on the wall, on which were two hooks fixed back to back and some distance apart; round them was fastened a thick crimson silk cord. As he unwound it, Alice saw that it communicated with a pulley in the ceiling over which it hung, and dangling from which was a bar of wood about two-and-a-half feet long—the cord dividing about three feet above it and being fastened to each of its ends.

"Now, Maud," said Sir Edward, "put her in position and fix her wrists."

Maud walked up to Alice and led her beneath the pulley. Sir Edward allowed the bar to descend to a level with the top of her shoulders. Maud then took the naked girl's right wrist and fastened it by a strap ready prepared to one end of the bar, so that the back of the hand was against it. And then she did the same with the left hand.

"Ready?" asked Sir Edward.

"Ready," answered Maud.

Whereupon he pulled the cord, availing himself of the hooks to get a purchase, until Alice's arms were stretched high above her head, and her whole body was well drawn up, the balls of her feet only resting on the floor.

"Oh, uncle! oh, uncle! oh, please! oh! not so high! oh! my arms will be dislocated! oh! it hurts my wrists!" and, involuntarily moving, she found very little would swing her off her feet.

Sir Edward, finding her sufficiently drawn up, fixed the cord, and, taking the whip in his right hand, played with the lash with his left as he gloated upon the exquisite naked girl—her extended arms, her shoulders, her breasts, her stomach, her navel, her abdomen, her back, her thighs, her buttocks, her legs, all displayed and glowing with shame and beauty.

At last, raising his whip, as he stood at her left, he said:—

"So we 'pea'd like a mare before uncle,' and are now going to be flogged like a mare."

Alice, in silent terror, drew up first one leg and then the other, showing off the exquisitely moulded limbs, and giving more than a glimpse of other charms.

"And," went on her uncle, "on the very part guilty of the offence." Whisp—whisple.

He had raised the whip, swinging out the lash, and brought it down with full force across the front of the girl's thighs, the lash striking her fair on the cunt. For a moment she was speechless, but the next emitted a piercing yell as she threw her head back and struggled to be free.

Sir Edward's arm was now across him.

Whisp, whisple went the whip as he gave the return stroke severely across her bottom, making her dance with anguish and leaving a red weal.

Whisp, whisple went the whip with merciless precision back again.

Alice's gymnastics were of the most frantic description. She jumped and threw out her legs and swung to and fro, showing every atom of her form, in utter recklessness of what she showed or of what she concealed.

When three strokes had been administered backwards and forwards from the left side, Sir Edward went round to the right—there her bottom received the forward and her front the back strokes, and well laid on they were. Sir Edward delighted in the infliction of a punishment which left his victim no reserve or concealment whatever, and he made the whip cut into the flesh.

Alice, almost suffocated with her cries and sobs, writhed for several minutes after the last stroke. At last her agony became less intense and her sobs fewer.

A high stool was then put before her and on it a po.

It was pushed close up to her, and Sir Edward inserted his hand from behind and tickled and frigged her cunt, saying:

"Yesterday you pea'd to please yourself. To-day you shall do so to please me."

Alice, beside herself, knew not what to do. She had not relieved herself since the night before. At last, with a shudder, a copious flood burst out, partly over her uncle's hand, and she gave a groan as she realized the manner in which she had been made to disgrace herself.

Her uncle then loosened the rope sufficiently to let her heels rest on the ground, and calling Maud to the sofa, which was immediately in front of Alice, he threw her back on it, while she quickly unfastened and pulled down his trousers, exposing his back view entirely to Alice. Maud, too, whose petticoats were up to her waist, threw wide her legs, and Sir Edward, prostrating himself upon her, fucked her violently before Alice.

Never was Alice so conscious of her nakedness as then.

Never, apparently, did Maud enjoy the pleasure of a good fucking more than she did in the presence of that naked and tied-up girl.

And never did Sir Edward acquit himself with greater prowess.

Alice's movements, as she saw her uncle's exertions in Maud's arms, and his strong, sinewy, bare and hairy legs, and his testicles hanging down, and heard his deep breathing and Maud's gasps and sighs— began again, but this time from pleasure instead of pain. She could not, however, as she longed to, get her hands to her cunt, and could only imitate the motions of the impassioned pair before her by a sympathetic movement to and fro—which expressed, but did not assuage her desires—and by little exclamations of longing.

At length the crisis was reached, and Sir Edward sank into Maud's embrace, while Alice could see, and imagined almost that she could *hear*, the throb, throb, throb that was sending thrill after thrill through Maud, and was causing her such a transport of delight that she seemed about to faint from it.

And then he untied her, and was about to leave them, when Alice said, in a most bewitching way:—

"Could you not 'fuck' (a deep blush) me—just once, dear uncle?"

Her half-closed eyes, her splendid form, her nakedness, reawakened her uncle's love and re-invigorated his bestowal of those sensible proofs of it in which ladies so delight. He replied:

"Maud has made me work pretty hard, my dear; but," putting one hand upon her shoulder as she faced him, "as you honour me with such a command, I should be but a *fainéant* and ungallant knight were I not to execute it—or at any rate to make an effort to do so," added he, leading the beautiful girl, nothing loth, to the couch whereon he had enjoyed Maud and gently pushing her backwards, amid her cries and exclamations and involuntary but pretty reluctance, inserted himself into her embrace. She inundated him once, and Maud, perceiving it, slipped her hand between his thighs. This help, good at need, soon worked the cavalier up to a proper appreciation of the situation in which he lay, and to a due expression of his sense of it; to the lady's intense gratification especially, as her forces were sufficient to enable her to, a second time—and this time at exactly the right instant—

Tumble down,
And break her crown

and, fortunately, *not* "come tumbling after" Jack, as Jill does in the story.

Although her uncle gave her these marks of affection, yet he did not relent in severity. She was kept without drawers the whole fortnight—a severe punishment! And the stiff white petticoats kept what skirts she had well off her legs, so that when she was seated could not fail to be seen.

And, indeed, after the lashing on the trapeze, she was not allowed to resume that day any garments at all.

She had been given a notebook in which she was compelled to make an entry of every fault and the punishment she was to receive for it.

In her room, on that particular day, aghast at her own nakedness, and thinking herself alone, she had taken up a pair of drawers which, by accident or design, were left there—she had gone to get ready for luncheon—and put them on, when suddenly Sir Edward entered the room.

"What do you mean, miss, by putting on those things? Did I not tell you you were to remain naked the whole of to-day?"

"I only put them on for a moment. I felt so ashamed of being naked."

"Take out your book and write:— For being ashamed of being naked, and for disobedience to my uncle, I am to ask him to give me two dozen with the tawse across his knee after supper this evening, and I am to remain stark naked for three days."

"Oh! oh! oh! Forgive me, dear uncle. I won't be ashamed any more. I won't disobey you any more. I won't indeed."

But it was no use.

At luncheon she had to sit down naked. All the afternoon she had to go about so. If only she might have had one scrap of clothing on! At dinner she could not dress, absolutely naked again; not even shoes or slippers permitted. And that to last three days more! All the evening naked; and as she thought of it she rolled over on to the pillow of the couch and hid her face; but, notwithstanding, felt naked still.

After supper came those terrible two dozen with the tawse. The tawse is a Scotch instrument of punishment, and in special favour with Scotch ladies, who know how to lay it on soundly. It is made of a hard and seasoned piece of leather about two feet long, narrow in the handle and at the other end about four inches broad, cut into narrow strips from about six to nine inches in length.

Alice had never seen, much less felt one.

She was commanded to bring it to her uncle, and had to go for it naked—not even a fan was allowed! How could she conceal the least of her emotions? Oh, this nakedness was an awful, awful thing!

She brought it, and opened her book and knelt down and said:

"Please, uncle, give me two dozen with the tawse for being ashamed and trying to cover my nakedness, and for my disobedience."

"Across my knee."

"Across—your—knee."

"Very well. Get up. Stand sideways close up to me. Now," taking the tawse in his right hand and putting his left arm round her waist, "lean right down, your head on the carpet, miss," and holding her legs with his left one, he slowly and deliberately laid on her sore bottom two dozen well-applied stripes. Then letting her go, she rolled sprawling on the carpet with pain and exhaustion.

The three days' nakedness were rigorously enforced.

They entirely overcame and quenched every spark of shame that was left about her, and she was much the more charming. Her silly simplicity, her country ignorance, were replaced by an artless coquetry and a self-possession which took away the breath and struck those in her presence with irresistible admiration.

Other punishments, too, she had to endure, some of them of a fantastic character.

The fortnight passed rapidly; but the last week, during which she was mistress, was a trying one for her. The servants scarcely heeded a baby in short frocks, with bare legs except for her long stockings, and became careless.

Many a smacking she received across her uncle's knee in the dining-room, or wherever they might happen to be, for some shortcoming; often was she sent away hungry from the table and locked up in a black hole for hours because she had not ordered this or that, or someone had done what he disapproved of. And after supper every evening, and all night if he was in the humour, she was required to be at his disposal and to give him pleasure in every form his endless ingenuity could invent.

At the end of the week, when her drawers were restored to her, she scarcely cared for them; but had not worn them long when the recollection of having been so much without them gave her the sweetest sense of shame possible.

CHAPTER VI

THE END

Quoth she, "Before you tumbled me
You promised me to wed."
—Old Song

So life continued for a long while at Bosmere Hall. The summer ripened into autumn; winter followed, and then spring, when, on good authority, it is said the thoughts turn to love.

The hunting had delighted Alice, notwithstanding that she had been once or twice soundly birched by her uncle in the open air for some error of the *ménage*, and made to ride home without trousers.

She came, however, to like these punishments; but one day she thought she had seriously offended him, for he declared his intention of marrying her to his heir. She would have preferred him.

The heir and she met at a ball. He was a charming young man. Alice's bashfulness had long departed. She recognized some likeness to her uncle—she knew his wishes. She waltzed five or six times with her cousin, who was intoxicated with her beauty and her short dress, her openwork stockings with the clocks at the side, the tiny little dancing shoes; the rosy flesh, and the perfume of love in every breath she exhaled.

They went together to supper, and afterwards retired to a distant conservatory. Soon his arm was about her, while his other hand was busily engaged, to her delight, underneath her petticoats. The honeyed phrases and sweet nothings that so please lovers followed, and they were to be married in three months. The period rapidly passed.

On her wedding day her uncle presented her with a hundred thousand pounds personal property of his own, which became her own, apart from her husband and the inheritance and settlements, and also with the famous cairn gorms.

Alice smiled and wept as brides will on her departure to spend Easter with her husband at Rome.

She taught him much, and, on the other hand, learned one or two things from him. But what surprised her most of all was that, whilst she often thought with ridicule and contempt of the days spent with her old aunt in Yorkshire, she always regarded with joy and satisfaction those spent at Bosmere Hall with her uncle and Maud, and felt she would ever consider them as the happiest of her life.

BIRCHGROVE PRESS
Flagellant & Libertine Erotica

———

Birchgrove Press specializes in producing new print and e-book editions of pre-1950s writings on sexual flagellation in English. Original editions of many of the books that we offer are difficult to obtain and are highly sought after. We are especially proud to offer new editions of rare Victorian flagellant texts such as *The Mysteries of Verbena House*, *Experimental Lecture by Colonel Spanker*, and *The Quintessence of Birch Discipline*. Birchgrove Press also produces new editions of libertine literature. We have published *Venus in the Cloister*, *The School of Venus*, *The Dialogues of Luisa Sigea*, and Isidore Liseux's translation of the Marquis de Sade's *Justine* (1791), *Opus Sadicum*, for example. For a full list of titles and formats, please visit our website:

www.birchgrovepress.com.